I0573264

Credits

Author
John Stater

Developers
Bill Webb

Producer
Bill Webb of Necromancer Games

Editor
Bill Webb of Necromancer Games

Layout and Production
Charles A. Wright

Front Cover Art
MKUltra Studios

Interior Art
Rowena Aitken

Cartography
Rick Sardinha

Playtesters
Frog God Games Staff

Special Thanks
Bill Webb would like to thank Bob Bledsaw and Bill Owen for inventing the original hex crawl — the standard in wilderness adventure and hours of fun.

FROG GOD GAMES

TOUGH ADVENTURES FOR TOUGH PLAYERS

Table of Contents

Hex Crawl Chronicles

— Valley of the Hawks —

By John Stater

The Valley of Hawks is a wooded river valley that cuts across a verdant prairie. It is named for the giant specimen of hawks that hunt along its banks and, during the Spring, blacken its skies. Three key rivers flow through the Valley of the Hawks, including the White River, the lesser Black River, and the Great River, which connects the Valley of the Hawks with the great trade centers of the northern lake country and the powerful cities of the southern coast.

In the days of myth and legend, the Valley of the Hawks was inhabited by a race of giants who carved their likenesses in stone and hunted monstrous creatures using the giant hawks as their ardent companions and helpers. In the shadow of the giant dwelled the trouping elves and their erstwhile goblin enemies, fighting and feasting and making sport of life. The coming of the golden men from the west sent the proud elves and vicious goblins into hiding, for they commanded powerful magics and built a grand city of metal and crystal. But the reach of the golden men exceeded their grasp, and within a few generations their city had fallen and sent its children into the valley as orphans, and the elves and goblins worked their vengeance on them until only a few bands of the golden men, as wild and savage as the beasts, still roam the Valley.

In recent times, two new groups of men have come to claim the Valley. The dusky-skinned miners from the northern lake country have ventured down the Great River to work the iron and coal deposits, while the dashing folk from the southern coast have ventured up the Great River to trade for furs and skins and fell the remaining forests of the Valley. The northmen arrived first, but their mines are almost worked out and their society has grown uninspired, and they have withdrawn from the White River in the face of the more aggressive southmen.

And so our adventurers arrive in the Valley of the Hawks seeking fame and fortune. Perhaps they come from northern lands or southern lands or perhaps they were born in the Valley and seek to learn its secrets and use its wealth to found a new city in the manner of the long gone golden men, a city that shines and terrifies and engraves their names forever in the stories of elves and men.

Valley of the Hawks is a hex-crawl, referring to the hex-shaped units that divide the map. Just as dungeon adventures take place on a gridded map, wilderness adventures can be conducted on a hex map, allowing players the freedom to decide where their characters roam and giving them the thrill of discovering the many places and people that have been placed on the map. This map represents a large area filled with numerous places to discover and explore, and can be used as a campaign area in its own right, or dropped into an existing campaign. Referees can place adventures they have purchased or devised on their own into empty hexes on the map.

Adventures in the Wilderness

The hexes on this map are 6 miles wide from one side to the other. In open country, adventurers should be able to see from one side of the hex to another. In wooded hexes, vision is much more restricted. Random encounters with monsters should be diced for each day and each night, with encounters occuring on the roll of 1-2 on 1d6. The exact monster (or monsters) encountered depends on the terrain through which the adventurers are traveling. Unlike dungeons, in which the monsters on the upper levels are usually less powerful than the monsters on deeper levels, wilderness encounters are quite variable in their challenge, and low level characters face death every time they step out of the confines of civilization. Well traveled adventurers will discover, however, that farmland and the river are not as dangerous as the highlands, swamp and woodlands.

Roll	Badlands	Grassland	Woodland
1	Bear, Cave (1d6)	Ankheg (1d4)	Ankheg (1d6)
2	Bird Men (2d6+6)	Bison (2d6+6)	Boar, Wild (1d6)
3	Giant, Hill (1d6)	Blink Dog (1d6)	Bugbear (2d6)
4	Goblin (2d6+20)	Bulette (1d3)	Dryad (1d6)
5	Gorgon (1d3)	Centaur (1d6)	Elf (2d6+6)
6	Harpy (2d6)	Goblin (2d6+10)	Goblin (2d6+10)
7	Hawk, Giant (1d8)	Hawk, Giant (1d6)	Hag, Annis (1d3)
8	Human, Berserker (2d6+10)	Human, Merchant (see below)	Hawk, Giant (1d6)
9	Manticore (1d6)	Human, Patrol (see below)	Owlbear (1d6)
10	Noroob (2d6)	Tiger, Sabre-Tooth (1d3)	Skunk, Giant (1d6)
11	Owlbear (2d6)	Wasp, Giant (1d4)	Stag, Giant (1d6)
12	Worg (2d6)	Wolf (2d6)	Wolf (2d6)

Use the stats for a giant eagle for the giant hawks.

Dwarves

A doughty band of dwarves have arrived recently in the Valley of the Hawks, conquering the upper levels of the Marble Domes (Hex 1616) and seeking bands of adventurers to help clear the lower galleries that they might mine the ancient tunnels for gems and precious metals. The dwarves are especially fond of smoke, and carry meerscheim pipes of great size and ornamentation as signs of their rank. Gifts of tobacco, especially blended pipe tobaccos, are a quick way to make friends among the dwarves (and enemies if the apportionment of the tobacco is not done just right). The dwarves rarely venture from their stronghold, preferring to allow human caravans to come to them with foodstuffs, tobacco and other items necessary for a comfortable life underground.

Elves

The native elves of the region are in the tradition of the trouping fairies – every elf a lord or lady in dazzling raiment of mauve, cyan and soft green, riding a fine horse and carrying ornate bows and long swords. They dwell in a hidden fort in Hex 0310, the fort being disguised by illusions and enchantments to look like a grassy knoll. The elves tend moontrees, whose leaves absorb moonlight that distills into the sap. Dead branches have a core of hardened sap which is melted down and alloyed with aluminum and tin to form elven mail. Their cloaks of elvenkind come from the silk of the faerie dragon, which lives in globes of spun silk that look like colored lanterns hanging from the trees. Their boots of elvenkind come from the hides of harts that are killed and slaughtered ritually to gain the blessing of the forest. The elves of the Valley are haughty and proud, but also terribly dashing and brave.

Men

As mentioned above, there are three societies of men in the Valley, none on terribly friendly terms with the others.

The **Golden Men** are descended from the ancients and now dwell in small hunter-gatherer bands in the woodlands or as brutal nomads on the prairie. They have golden-brown skin and blazing red hair. Warriors wear leather armor and carry stout clubs and leather slings, or metal weapons they have scavenged from their victims.

The **Northmen** have ebony or chocolate skin and wavy hair of brown or black, often worn long. Most are stout and plump, but a few villages mingled with the elves in elder times and are noted for their height and the electric sparkle in their eyes. The northmen are known for their baggy trousers and long tunics. They favor axes and curved knives and usually wear chainmail or platemail.

The **Southmen** have tan or olive skin and a great variety of hair and eye colors. They wear long, straight tunics and woolen leggings. Their shoes are leather and pointed, and they wear tall pointed hats with wide brims; both shoes and hats are decorated with buckles of brass or silver. The southmen carry long swords and daggers, and wear either ring armor or chainmail. Their leaders are skilled in swordsmanship and magic (treat them as elves), earning their followers the nickname of witchmen.

While most mercantile trade through this region is conducted via river, **caravans** move through the area regularly from the vast prairies to the south and west. Each caravan consist of 1d6 merchants, and each merchant has either 2d6 llamas loaded with packs or 1d6 wagons pulled by oxen. You can determine what is being carried by a llama or wagon using the chart below, using your best judgement to determine quantity. There are two guards per llama or five guards per wagon. The guards are mounted on horses, wear leather armor and carry shields, long swords and light crossbows.

Merchant: HD 1d6; AC 7 [12]; Atk 1 weapon (1d6); Move 12; Save 18; CL/XP B/10; Special: None.

Guard: HD 1; AC 6 [13]; Atk 1 weapon (1d8); Move 12 (18 on horseback); Save 17; CL/XP 1/15; Special: None.

Rumors

When adventurers are seeking information or rumors in a settlement or from the lord of a castle, you can roll a random rumor from the table below. Each rumor is either True ("T") or False ("F") and the hex number associated with the rumor is given in brackets.

Roll	Rumor	Roll	Rumor
1	The men of Gregar worship a dark divinity (T) **Hex 0125**	11	No good ever came from wading in a fountain or pool in the wilderness (T/F)
2	Beware the blue flames of Rhombus when plundering his tomb (T) **Hex 0301**	12	Utter no sound on the prairie, for you may awaken it and bring ruination on us all (T) **Hex 1602**
3	Those who sup with the elves may never return to the land of the living (F) **Hex 0310**	13	A gorgon lives in a misty ravine in the badlands (T) **Hex 1720**
4	Beware the maiden of the river's edge (T) **Hex 0504**	14	The very air of the Old city is poisonous (F) **Hex 1906**
5	The Monks of the Mute Contemplation flee from loud noises (F) **Hex 0605**	15	A lich plots red ruin beneath the Old City (T/F) **Hex 1906**
6	The monuments of the ancients are tainted by dark magic (F)	16	Kelban is wise beyond wisdom (T) **Hex 1918**
7	Awful things emerge from the woods at night (T) **Hex 0711**	17	Lord Mayor Tarset is not to be trusted (T) **Hex 2213**
8	The basalt lion means certain death (T) **Hex 0803**	18	A wicked giant yet dwells in the badlands (T) **Hex 2519**
9	Mushroom-men are harmless if offered beer (F) **Hex 1007**	19	The white elves are servants of Death (T) **Hex 2519**
10	The hospice of Almerla is a sanctuary from the elves (F) **Hex 1414**	20	They say Lord Djak is hiring mercenaries for a great campaign (T) **Hex 3210**

Random Caravan Goods

Roll	Goods
1	Armor (1-2 = leather, 3-4 = shields, 5 = chainmail, 6 = full plate)
2	Drink (ale, beer, spiced wine, spirits)
3	Foodstuffs (dried meat, fruit, grain, vegetables)
4	Silver Ingots (each ingot weighs 5 pounds and is thus worth 50 sp)
5	Spices (pepper, salt, saffron)
6	Weapons

Patrols are mostly from the town of Swiftwater. Each patrol contains 1d6+6 men-at-arms mounted on horses, wearing ring mail and carrying shield, lance, long sword and light crossbow. Each patrol is led by a sergeant wearing chainmail, but otherwise armed as his men.

Man-At-Arms: HD 1; AC 5 [14]; Atk 1 weapon (1d8); Move 9 (18 on horseback); Save 17; CL/XP 1/15; Special: None.

Sergeant: HD 3; AC 3 [16]; Atk 1 weapon (1d8); Move 9 (18 on horseback); Save 14; CL/XP 3/60; Special: None.

Encounter Key

0108. A quick sparkling stream flows through a wooded valley here. Rising above the leafy canopy one can make out an enormous tower keep of black stone and many plumes of black smoke rising to the heavens. The keep is owned by the warlord Agnach, a gap-toothed old soldier given to deep melancholies. He rules over a small village of northmen, coal miners and swineherds who do some boar hunting on the side. The miners live in sturdy houses of wood and stone and burn coal to keep warm. Agnach has under his command 30 longbowmen, five sergeants, 11 stout-hearted knights famed through the region for their bravery and charity and the cleric Morgis of the Deer-Eyes and the magic-user Gilma the White. The knights have recently become restless, as they have seen their formerly honorable lord descend into irrationality and paranoia. Not two weeks ago, Agnach imprisoned his only daughter, Bertilda (who, though generous and gregarious, sadly resembles her father) in one tower of his stronghold, claiming that an army of shadows is haunting the woods and means to take her away. Each night, he sends his archers into the woods with lanterns to frighten away the shadows. The truth of his affliction lies in the sealed up torture chambers beneath the keep. Agnach took his stronghold from the magic-user known as The Forgotten One [Hex 1309], who he sent into bitter exile. The Forgotten One has concocted a strain of semi-intelligent rope-like fungus that has now colonized the torture chamber and releases spores that are slowly driving the inhabitants of the castle mad.

Treasure: 1,900 cp, 4,270 gp and a piece of amber worth 5 gp.

Agnach, Fighter Lvl 9: HP 40; AC 1 [18]; Save 6, CL/XP 9/1100. Platemail, shield, +1 spear that sheds light in a 15' radius, dagger. Curly red hair, brown eyes, golden-brown skin, pudgy with a pug-nosed face.

Morgis of the Deer-Eyes, Cleric Lvl 4: HP 13; AC 4 [15]; Save 12 (10 vs. paralysis and poison); CL/XP 5/240; Special: Cast up to 2nd level spells, turn undead. Chainmail, shield, mace. Willowy, light-skinned man with thinning chestnut hair and large eyes. He is abrupt and always on the move, and enjoys solving puzzles. Morgis is married to Gilma the White and has two children, Cruen and Justa. He worships Eosinn, the goddess of hunters, who appears as a tall female faun with grey eyes.

Gilma the White, Magic-User Lvl 6: HP 18; AC 9 [10]; Save 10 (8 vs. spells); CL/XP 7/600; Special: Can cast 3rd level spells. Pudgy, ivory-skinned woman with shoulder-length, platinum hair. She has a keen interest in exotic plants (keeping a small greenhouse with orchids and a few deadly plant creatures near the village).

0125. There is a palisaded village of northmen iron miners here, northmen living in thatched houses. The palisade is surrounded by a dry moat filled with shards of iron and globs of slag. The villagers have wide faces and wiry builds, arm themselves with picks and throwing axes and don chainmail and shields in times of trouble. Whether it is the effect of the strange water of their reservoir or their worship of Narulhaq (see below), the villagers are capable of generating Darkness 15 ft Radius at will.

The village is ruled by Big Berta, an imposing woman miner who is officially the village mayor, but really the village bully. The miners get their water from a nearby reservoir (a former quarry), and the water has a weird, metallic taste. Overlooking the reservoir is a small, crooked tower that serves as the home of Shatshan the Wise, a sage and priest of a weird deity called Narulhaq. Narulhaq has the body of an old man and the head of a wasp, with blue eyes like sapphires and wearing a coat of human bones. Narulhaq's shrine is located beneath the tower in a small, circular chamber with a flooded floor. Here, Shatshan drown sacrificial victims, adding their bones to the idol's coat. Shatshan is married to Riatha, a handsome lass from the village in Hex 116. Riatha's father was forced into agreeing to the marriage by Cloda, who gets shipments of blood from Shatshan once a month. Riatha is miserable, and is desperate to escape her strange, old husband.

Treasure: 170 gp, 1,000 sp, a hematite worth 700 gp and a terracotta brazier decorated with acanthus leaves worth 65 gp and kept in the shrine of Narulhaq.

Big Berta: HD 2+2 (11 hp); AC 9 [10] or 5 [14] in armor; Atk 1 fist (1d2+1) or weapon (1d6+1); Move 12; Save 16; CL/XP 2/30; Special: Darkness 15' Radius. Berta is an imposing woman who is knowledgeable about horses and is never far from her pick. She wears an orichalcum armband worth 115 gp.

Shatshan the Sage: HD 2 (10 hp); AC 9 [10]; Atk 1 weapon (1d4); Move 12; Save 16; CL/XP 3/60; Special: Darkness 15' Radius, can cast 1st level cleric and magic-user spells. A cold-hearted villain, Shatshan pretends to be sociable and friendly. He has a fragile build, fair skin, brown eyes and grey hair, and a long, mournful face.

0202. A small village of thrifty woodsmen sits near the banks of the river amidst the rugged, wooded hills. The woodsmen topple oaks and send the timber down river on barges to Swiftwater. The village is composed of wattle & daub longhouses and is surrounded by a wooden palisade with a soggy moat and watch towers. The woodsmen are very tall and have thick, wavy auburn hair, blue-grey eyes and creamy brown skin. Their narrow faces, thin noses and large eyes mark them as kin to the elves, and their elf-blood allows them to live within the woods without harrassment from the elves or most other fey. In times of war, the woodsmen are expert longbowmen and wear leather armor and carry short swords. The village is governed by Illheard the Reeve, appointed by the Lord Mayor of Swiftwater,

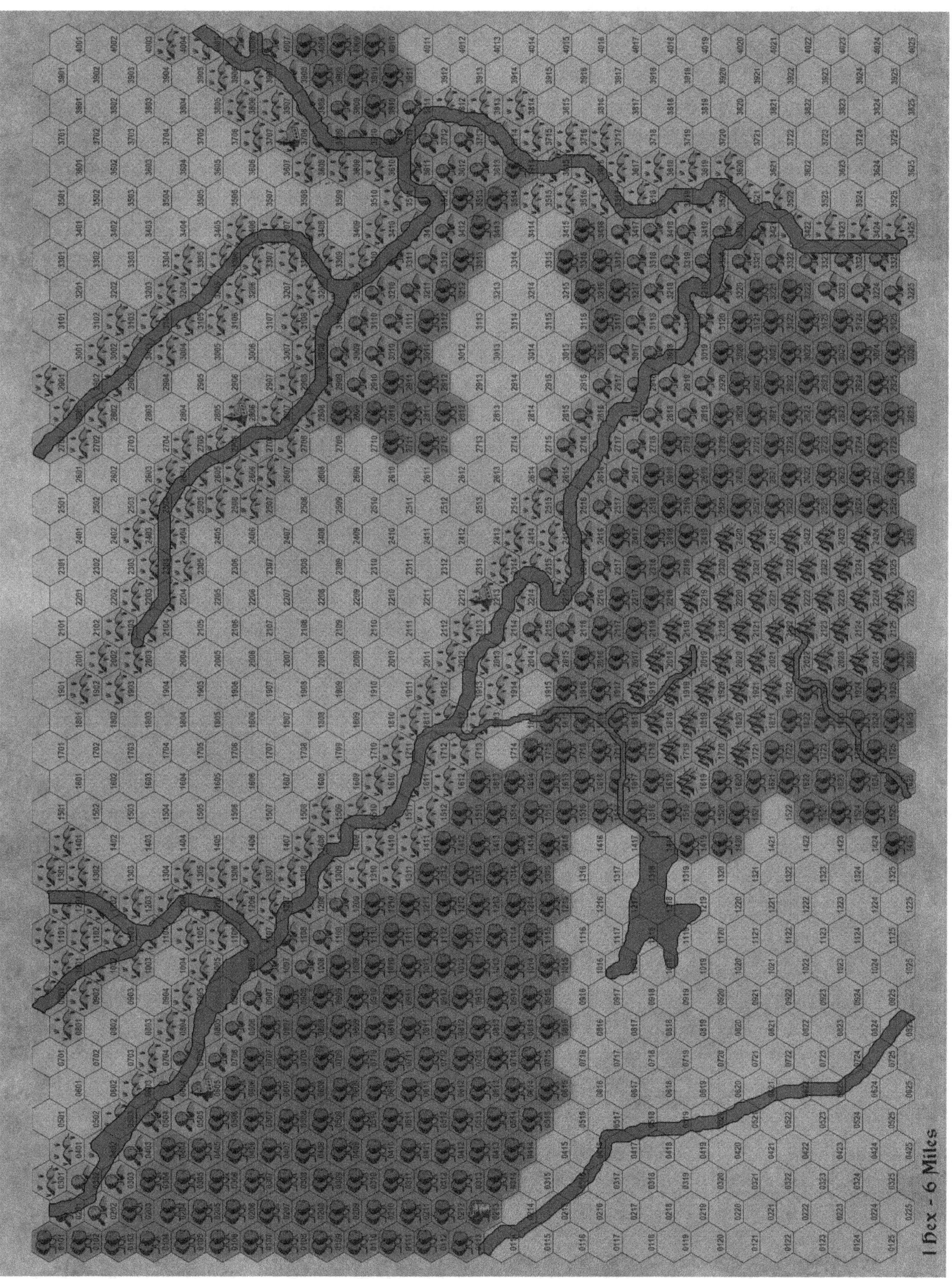
1 Hex - 6 Miles

to which the woodsmen pay a hated tribute. The village has a shrine to the healing goddess Almerla [Hex 0411] run by Charl the Mild.

Treasure: 1,900 cp, 2,600 sp, 1,420 gp (hidden in the shrine) and a turquoise worth 105 gp.

Illheard the Reeve: HD 3 (20 hp); AC 7 [12] in armor; Atk 1 weapon (1d6); Move 12; Save 14; CL/XP 3/60; Special: None. Illheard dons leather armor and carries a short sword in times of trouble. She is a small woman with tan skin, a thin face, black hair and tan eyes. A perfumer by trade, she harvests fragrant river lillies to make scents that she sends back to Sweetwater with the timber shipments. She is passive and gracious by nature, and is the younger sister of Lord Mayor Tarset of Sweetwater.

Charl the Mild: HD 5 (14 hp); AC 9 [10]; Atk 1 weapon (1d8); Move 12; Save 12; CL/XP 5/240; Special: Scores double damage when surprises a foe, surprises on 1-3 on 1d6. Charl is an assassin posing as a priest. Charl appears sweet-natured and reserved, and has tan skin, blue-grey eyes, brown hair and a long, knowing face. He always keeps three daggers hidden on his person.

0213. The arch-transmogrifier Cloda has established her tower in this hex. Cloda's tower is constructed of white marble and looks like two stacked cubes, each measuring about forty feet on each side, topped by a tall array of tubes and wires. It has no windows and no apparent door, although there is a large secret door on the north side. The tower's interior is a maze of passages, stairs (some leading nowhere) and small chambers. Near the pinnacle of the tower, Cloda keeps a library and beneath the tower a laboratory containing a large, silver oven. Cloda is the originator of owlbears in the region (hers are a cross of black bears and great horned owls, and although smaller than the norm are quicker and more clever) and has created several other crossbreeds in her mystic oven, which is powered by mercury, blood and distilled dreamstuff. Cloda collects dreamstuff using the weird array of wires atop the tower, the wires collecting the dreams of the surrounding villagers and dripping it into silver vials. The silvery dreamstuff is useful in magical research, but if consumed gives one terrible nightmares and may cause madness.

Cloda's tower is surrounded by a large village of vigorous, though foppish, southmen living in stone cottages. The village is constructed on terraces surrounding the tower and protected by stone wall and a small gatehouse. The village has an expert bowyer named Sleig. The villagers have heavy, iron doors on their homes and keep them bolted and barred at night, for the mistress allows her pets to roam freely (3 in 6 chance of encountering one at night in this hex).

Cloda is assisted by two apprentices, Gilos and Carazzo.

Treasure: 3,460 gp, 1,500 sp, tiger's eye gem worth 115 gp and three tiger skins worth 25 gp each.

Cloda, Magic-User 9: HP 26; AC 9 [10]; Save 7 (5 vs. spells); CL/XP 11/1700; Special: Can cast 5th level spells. She is short, fanatical about cleanliness, big-boned and pale-skinned, with golden brown hair kept in a bun. She loves books, and has a collection of elven love poetry. Wears workman's clothes and carries a silver dagger.

Gilos, Magic-User Lvl 2: HP 4; AC 9 [10]; Save 14 (12 vs. spells); CL/XP 3/60; Special: Can cast 1st level spells. He is straightforward and flirtatious, with fair skin, hazel eyes, black hair and a heavy, round face. He loves riddles and considers himself an expert.

Carazzo, Magic-User Lvl 2: HP 2; AC 9 [10]; Save 14 (12 vs. spells); CL/XP 3/60; Special: Can cast 1st level spells. He is slight of frame, with a thin face, nearly black skin and hazel eyes. Carazzo is fanatical in his devotion to Mana-Yood-Sushai

(Hex 0605) and a bit scatterbrained – he has been known to cast spells (randomly) he should not know. He is the son of a large family in Swiftwater.

You can use the following weird cross-breeds as random encounters in this hex:

1 — Hyaven: HD 1; AC 7 [12]; Atk 1 bite (1d3); Move 16; Save 17; CL/XP 2/30; Special: None. Looks like a hyena with the legs and wings of a large raven.

2 — Bulleopard: HD 3+1; AC 6 [13]; Atk 1 gore (1d6), 1 bite (1d6), 2 claws (1d3); Move 18; Save 14; CL/XP 4/120; Special: None. Looks like a bull with the coloration, head and claws of a leopard.

3 — Owlbear: HD 5+1; AC 5 [14]; Atk 2 claws (1d6), 1 bite (2d6); Move 12; Save 12; CL/XP 5.240; Special: Hug for additional 2d8 if to-hit roll is 18+.

4 — Gazasp: HD 2; AC 4 [15]; Atk 1 bite (1d3 + poison), gore (1d3); Move 18; Save 16; CL/XP 3/60; Special: Poison (save or die). Looks like a gazelle with the fangs and tail of an asp.

5 — Hedgelion: HD 5; AC 4 [15]; Atk 2 claws (1d6), 1 bite (1d8); Move 12 (Burrow 6); Save 12; CL/XP 5/240; Special: None. Looks like a bulky lion covered in the spikes of a hedgehog with an overlong snout and large claws fit for digging.

6 — Eleparrot: HD 10; AC 6 [13]; Atk 1 bite (1d10); 2 trample (2d8); Move 12; Save 5; CL/XP 11/1700; Special: None. Looks like an elephant with the face and talons of a parrot and brighly colored feathers.

0221. A large granite hillock in this hex serves as the home of Talldesa, an oread. An oread is a dryad that merges with stone instead of wood. Talldesa can speak with the stones in this region, sending messages via stones to the wizards of the region and receiving messages back. She is also a good source of rumors. Her hillock is surrounded by dozens of warty toads that she refers to as her "chorus". She can often be found loungin on her hillock listening to the croaking toads and the whispers of the stones.

Oread: HD 2 (7 hp); AC 6 [13]; Atk 1 stone dagger (1d4); Move 12; Save 16; CL/XP 3/60; Special: Charm person (-2 to the save).

0301. Here lies the tomb of Rhombus the Blessed, an ancient patriarch of Sclarad, the god of justice, who was interred here by his followers over 300 years ago. The tomb is a vault of stone covered by a man-made hill. A heavy stone blocks the entrance. Inside there is a sarcophagus made of iron and trapped with scything blades (saving throw or suffer 1d8 damage and lose 3 points of movement for the next week). Overlooking the sarcophagus is an iron idol of Sclarad. Sclarad looks like short, thin man with sapphire eyes (worth 100 gp), iron skin and dressed in aquamarine armor. The idol holds a +1 man-catcher. Piled around the tomb are a three suits of platemail, four coats of chainmail, a dozen shields and numerous other weapons, all of the finest quality but not magical. In a secret compartment of the sarcophagus there is 800 cp, 220 gp, a pearl worth 600 gp and an iron box holding 10 pounds of salt. The tomb is protected by six lambent blue flames that hover in mid-air and try to engulf a person's head. If successful, they control the person, sending them into a berserk rage against their comrades.

Blue Flames of Sclarad: HD 3; AC 3 [16]; Atk none; Move (Fly 18); Save 14; CL/XP 5/240; Special: Control minds, cause fury, only harmed by magic weapons and spells.

0310. The elf lord Cunobellis has his keep here, disguised as a hillock covered in clover and daffodils and topped by a single, large oak. For those who can pierce the illusion, the stronghold looks a round shell keep of white stone with a crenellated roof flying a dozen brightly-colored pennons. The gate into the keep is forged of bronze. The keep houses 60 elf men, women and children. The courtyard is an open air great hall, protected by tarps of blue, crimson and vert and featuring a stately throne of white wood decorated with tiles of malachite. Lord Cunobellis rules beside his wife, Lady Ysabel and has five champions named Aleach, Culiann, Faladh, Guoldis and Wibold. The elves pass the time feasting and playing, or riding out into the woods to hunt or simply parade. They are servants of the Spring Court, and thus mostly gentle and benign, but they have little patience for men or dwarves just the same.

Treasure: 26,610 sp, 2,000 gp.

Cunobelis, Elf Lvl 11: HP 64 / 24; AC 4 [15]; Save 4 / 5 (3 vs. spells); CL/XP 13/2300; Special: Can cast 5th level spells as magic-user. Elven chainmail, longsword, longbow, potion of healing. Peach skin, grey eyes, auburn hair in braids. A hunter extraordinary, it is almost all he talks about.

Champions, Elves Lvl 5: HP 30 / 12; AC 4 [15]; Save 11 / 12 (10 vs. spells); CL/XP 6/400; Special: Can cast 2nd level spells as magic-user. Elven chainmail, longsword, longbow.

0406. There is a tall, grey tower here in the woods. The interior is painted in a black and white checker pattern, like a chess board. A giant spider called Glom lives in the tower and challenges visitors to games of chess using zombie pieces. Her wager is simple – a person's life against a pair of slippers that allow one to spider climb. It's a poor wager, for the slippers wear out after a month. Glom has complete control over her zombies.

Glom: HD 4+2 (23 hp); AC 4 [15]; Atk 1 bite (1d6+2 + poison); Move 12; Save 13; CL/XP 7/600; Special: Poison (save or die), webs.

Zombies (32): HD 2; AC 7 [12]; Atk 1 weapon or strike (1d8); Move 6; Save 16; CL/XP 2/30; Special: Immune to sleep and charm.

0414. A tribe of 150 kill-bunnies has dug its burrows in this hex. The kill-bunnies wear garish war paint on their white bodies and arm themselves with cruel, barbed darts and axes. The trbe is commanded by Thogantel, who keeps a harem of ten does who are skilled as scouts and thieves. The kill-bunnies have been raiding pilgrim caravans headng for the Abbey of St. Almerla in Hex 0411. They know of Ishosausis in Hex 0512 and will lead adventurers into its lair if given the chance.

Treasure: 1,400 cp, 7,100 sp, 1,860 gp, a bronze trencher worth 150 gp and a sard worth 500 gp.

Kill-Bunny: HD 1; AC 5 [14]; Atk 1 bite (1d3) or 1 weapon (1d6); Move 15; Save 17; CL/XP 2/30; Special: Lightning reflexes, murderous rage.

Kill-Bunny Doe: HD 2; AC 4 [13]; Atk 1 bite (1d3) or 1 weapon (1d6); Move 15; Save 16; CL/XP 3/60; Special: Lightning reflexes, murderous rage, double damage during surprise, fascinate creatures with dances.

Thogantel: HD 3 (10 hp); AC 3 [16]; Atk 1 bite (1d4) or 1 weapon (1d8); Move 15; Save 14; CL/XP 4/120; Special: Lightning reflexes, murderous rage.

0504. Over 200 years ago, a wise woman of the elves drowned in the river here, killed by a prince whose affections she spurned. Her spirit became a rusalka, a undead being that seeks vengeance on the living. Belena appears as a comely elf shrouded in fog and mist. Upon closer inspection, she looks like a cadaver with burning, green eyes, eyes that cast a Charm Person spell on the unwary. Those who are charmed by her eyes are led into the river to drown. The touch of the creature paralyzes. Women slain by the rusalka rise as new rusalka the next night under the control of their creator. Rusalkas are repulsed by holy symbols and absinth.

Treasure: At the bottom of the river, hidden under a large stone, is 1,600 gp and a turquoise worth 200 gp.

Rusalka: HD 4+3 (20 hp); AC 3 [16]; Atk 1 bite (special); Move 9 (Swim 18); Save 13; CL/XP 8/800; Special: Charm, paralyze, drown victims, immune to non-magic weapons and mind-effecting spells, create a wall of fog.

0509. There is a grove of elven moontrees here tended by a druid called Wulfwin and guarded by a dozen elven archers.

Wulfwin: HD 8 (33 hp); AC 9 [10]; Atk 1 weapon (1d6) or spell; Move 12; Save 8; CL/XP 10/1400; Special: Shape change 3/day into an animal, cast 6th level magic-user spells and 8th level cleric spells. Wears a leopard skin cape worth 50 gp and has a jasper worth 500 gp.

Elves: HD 1+1; AC 3 [16]; Atk 1 sword (1d8) or 2 arrows (1d6); Move 12; Save 17; CL/XP 1/15; Special: None. Wear elven chainmail and carry longbows and longswords.

0524. An old, abandoned mine shaft is set in the side of a barren hillock. Rubble tumbles from the mine's opening to the stream that flows below. Climbing down the shaft, one can see a number of inferior rose quartzes jutting from the sides. At the bottom of the shaft, the mine turns into a series of low tunnels that eventually run into large, deep caverns, with better quality rose quartzes still embedded in the walls. The rose quartzes are all part of a silicon-based lifeform with impressive mental powers. It is attempting to understand carbon-based life by generating all manner of bizarre illusions (per Phantasmal Force, save at -4) and seeing how people react. The entity cares little whether its test subjects survive the experience. Attempts at mining in the mine are met with waves of psychic force that inflict 1d6 points of intelligence damage. At 0 intelligence, people become vegetables and eventually die of thirst. Intelligence lost in this manner will return at the rate of 1 point per day.

0605. The Palace of Mute Contemplation overlooks the river here. The "palace" is really a monastery of greenish-grey granite composed of a square structure with four tall towers topped with golden domes. The lands around the monastery are studded with tall, iron poles topped by silver godheads that have had a permanent Silence effect with a range of 300 yards cast upon them. These poles becomes more dense as one approaches the monastery, and the interior of the monastery has dozens of these heads hanging by chains from the ceiling with the same Silence spell cast upon them. The monastery has an inner sanctum barred by iron doors that are always locked and bolted shut. The monks, known for being zealots and assassins, dwell beneath the temple in catacombs along with their revered dead. The monks worship Mana-Yood-Sushai, who they believe has dreamed all creation, and that awakening him will mean the end of everything. To this end, they are dedicated to stamping out all sound, starting with the Valley of the Hawks and eventually silencing the entire universe. Obviously, their grasp on reality is a bit weak, so one must take care when dealing with them. The leader of the monks has no known name (or he has never spoken it). He and his brothers dress in brown robes tied with rope. They permit no metal in their domain.

Treasure: 700 cp, 640 sp, 1,160 gp, blocks of cinnamon wrapped in wax paper (10 lb, worth 10 gp per pound)

Abbot: HD 8; AC 3 [16]; Atk 3 strikes (1d8); Move 18; Save 8; CL/XP 9/1100; Special: Can cast Silence three times per day, strikes that deal maximum damage stun for 1d6 rounds.

Monks (20): HD 2; AC 7 [12]; Atk 2 strikes (1d8); Move 15; Save 16; CL/XP 3/60; Special: Can cast Silence once per day, strikes that deal maximum damage stun for 1d4 rounds.

0615. An old circle of stone menhirs stands atop a gently sloping hill. The circle shows signs of a recent camp, with tracks leading off in a random direction. Clerics who camp in this stone circle have a 1% chance of seeing visions in their dreams (per the Contact Other Plane spell).

0711. This hex contains a dungeon built by the ancient elves to house a slumbering entity of chaos. The dungeon consists of old tunnels excavated by purple worms. The entrance is barred by adamantine bars set into a circular gate. The gate is surrounded by bas-reliefs of sinuous mermaids and will only open when a hand signal is flashed by a magic-user of at least 3rd level. The proper hand signal can be found on the fountain in Hex 0914.

The upper level of the dungeon consists of wide tunnels and numerous small side passages. The tunnels are patrolled by an old purple worm, grey oozes and tick-like kobolds that feed on the worm and gather the valuable minerals excreted by it as it digs ands re-digs the upper tunnels.

The inner portion of the dungeon is a dome of adamantine with circular entry ports guarded by slug-like sphinxes that ask geometric riddles. The inner halls are roamed by the chaos creatures, mutated humanoids and random emotions that look like colored clouds of energy. The heart of the complex is a well of chaos lined with primordium, an ur-metal which can be used to forge chaos weapons and wands that enhance spells in dangerous, unpredictable ways. The metal is unstable, and can unleash primal energies that mutate living beings or turn creatures into random objects or objects into random creatures. Within the well of chaos creatures that looks like the fevered afterthoughts of a mad genius are born and often consumed within seconds. Some of these creatures escape to wander the halls of the dungeon.

0721. There are natural hot springs in this hex that produce a mild healing effect (double natural healing for those who spend an hour a day bathing in them). The stones around the springs are crusted with salts of every color under the sun, and the grasses around the springs have a purple hue. Living in these tall grasses is a community of salty little gnomes. The gnomes look like miniature dwarves covered in salt crystals and wearing pointed white hats. They are dour little men, and resist intrusions into their territory unless bribed with gifts. The gnomes wield poisoned picks (save or 1d6 damage). There are 50 such gnomes dwelling around the spring.

Salty Gnomes: HD 1d4; AC 6 [13]; Atk 1 pick (1d4 + poison); Move 6; Save 18; CL/XP B/10; Special: Phantasmal force 1/day, immune to poison and disease.

0803. Ishosausis is a bizarre entity that makes its home here in a scarp field marked with a few burnt boulders. The ground here is always smoky and a noxious haze fills the area (like a half-power Stinking Cloud) unless high winds blow it away. As one moves closer to the center of the field, they notice little pools of blood on the ground and an indistinct shape ahead. As the smoke clears a bit, they will see the statue of a lion in basalt, with ruby eyes. The statue rests in a little pool of blood and holds a silver sword in its jaws. As the adventurers approach, they will notice a woman walking towards them. The woman is beautiful, but rather thin, with crimson skin and long, black hair. She looks sad, and is dressed in rags of grey and black. This woman will ask the adventurers what they seek, and unless they answer "Wisdom" or something similar, she, Ishosausis, will take on her true form and attack. In her true form, Isoshausis, the spirit of violence, looks like an emaciated moose without antlers and drenched in blood. Her legs are twisted and bent, and her face writhes in spasms of agony. Upon closer scrutiny, you notice that her legs, which appear almost lifeless, are not touching the ground, and in fact this abortion of reason floats in mid-air.

Ishosausis: HD 14 (hp); AC 9 [10]; Atk 1 bite (1d10 + wisdom drain), 1 tail (1d10); Move (Fly 36); Save 3; CL/XP 12/2000; Special: Inflicts 2d8 when it beats its opponent's AC by 4 or more, bite drains 1 point of Wisdom, insubstantial, so only harmed by magic weapons and spells, creature's constant gaze forces victim to pass a saving throw or shrink to half its normal size for 1d4+1 turns – note, only the person will shrink, not their equipment.

0902. An abbey to Thallos, the god of love, has been built here in the woods on a granite cliff overlooking an idyllic meadow of tall, cool grasses and pale lavender wild flowers. The abbey is a structure of white marble and copper verdigris and looks like a mass of stumpy, round towers with tall, conical roofs. Set into the cliffs beneath the abbey are a dozen cave dwellings inhabited by halfling shepherds. The halflings keep tiny sheep on the meadow. The abbey is ruled by Bragni, a strapping, athletic centaur hedonist who welcomes visitors to indulge in wine, women and song. Women are provided by raids made by his centaur and halfling followers into surrounding villages, the captives being drugged and sometimes enchanted into becoming heirodules of Thallos. Bragni has developed a powerful desire for Illheard of Hex 0202, and is hatching a plan to kidnap her from the village. Thallos takes the form of a young man with a tall, angular build, hairless with seven red eyes, four wings and wearing a crown of glory.

Treasure: 1,500 sp, 6,200 gp and a gold idol of Thallos worth 7,200 gp set with seven carnelian eyes worth 15 gp each.

Bragni, Centaur Cleric Lvl 10: HP 38; AC 4 [15]; Atk 1 mace (1d6+1), 2 kicks (1d6); Move 18; Save 6 (4 vs. paralysis and poison); CL/XP 12/2000; Special: Can cast 5th level spells, turn undead. Shield, mace.

Centaurs (16): HD 4; AC 4 [16]; Atk 2 kicks (1d6) and weapon (1d8); Move 18; Save 13; CL/XP 5/240; Special: None.

Halflings (30): HD 1d6; AC 7 [12]; Atk 1 sling or sword (1d6); Move 6; Save 18; CL/XP B/10; Special: None.

0914. A moss-covered statued fountain rests here in a dense copse of twisted oaks. The statue is a plaintive mermaid with a bit of silver inlay still evident on her scales. The statue's nose and right arm have been chipped away, but her left arm and hand are still there, the hand in the mystic shape that opens the gate to the dungeon in Hex 0711.

1007. A band of 25 mushroom-men live in this hex. The mushroom-men resemble dryad's saddles, with wide, kidney-shaped flat heads with coloration reminiscent of a pheasant's feathers. The mushroom-men are tree dwellers, living in the branches in nests of packed, dried mud and twigs. The mushroom-men use nets to capture interlopers, selling them to the Forgotten One [Hex 1309]. When a mushroom-man dies, it releases 1d6 spores which rapidly grow into mushroom-men with one fewer hit dice than their parent. Mushroom-men with only 1 HD do not produce these spores. Assume that all of the encountered mushroom-men have 3 HD.

Treasure: 800 cp, 520 sp, 3,000 gp

Mushroom-Man: HD 3; AC 5 [14]; Atk Fist (1d6) or weapon; Move 12; Save 14; CL/XP 5/240; Special: Spores.

Mushroom-Man: HD 2; AC 5 [14]; Atk Fist (1d6) or weapon; Move 12; Save 16; CL/XP 3/60; Special: Spores.

Mushroom-Man: HD 1; AC 5 [14]; Atk Fist (1d6) or weapon; Move 12; Save 17; CL/XP 1/15; Special: Spores.

1022. Rising from the rolling landscape are a cluster of marble domes carved from marble outcroppings. The domes have secret entrances into a deep set of copper mines now owned by a clan of 300 dwarves and their 130 wives and 70 children. The dwarves are led by King Verion and his Iron Circle, a band of warrior-priests who enforce a spartan discipline on the dwarfs. The dwarves have wrested the upper mines from hobgoblins in league with hags, but the deeper mines still hold many dangers, and raids from bugbears are becoming ever more common. It is said that the deepest pit of the mine is home to a demon. King Verion is becoming hard pressed to protect his people, and the dwarves are becoming irritable from being pressed into a limited area.

1119. The fishermen of this village are descendants of the ancient men, having dark, golden skin and wavy red hair. Skilled animal handlers, they keep a pride of seven sabre-tooth tigers as guard animals under the control of seven chosen maidens, who form a sort of priesthood under the tutelage of the priestess Cimar. The village is technically run by Orloc (5 hp), its chief elder, an unassuming, good natured man. Recently, though, it came under the domination of a mercenary captain called Xaviennon, a tall man with a craggy face and cold eyes. Folk whisper that demon blood flows through his veins. Xaviennon commands 20 two-handed sword wielding horsemen in chainmail byrnies, who are all that remains after a disastrous campaign against Cloda in Hex 0213.

Cimar, Cleric Lvl 3: HP 14; AC 3 [16]; Save 13 (11 vs. paralysis and poison); CL/XP 4/120; Special: Can cast 2nd level spells, turn undead. A fanatic, she expects her god, Janan god of alchemy, will deliver the village from the depredations of

Xaviennon. Janan appears as a bat-winged youth, inhumanly tall and drawn, with emerald skin and curly black hair, wearing purple robes and a gold brooch. Janan holds a human skull and jackals are sacred to him.

Xaviennon, Fighting-Woman Lvl 7: HP 40; AC 2 [17]; Save 7; CL/XP 7/600. Platemail, two-handed sword. Stubborn and ruthless, keeps hunting falcons.

1306. A small village of stone cottages surrounded by an earthen rampart here supports about 100 bison hunters. The villagers are commanded by an infamous fighting-woman named Shard, recently dismissed from the army of Swiftwater. Besides their hunting, the villagers tend orchards of red, delicious apples along the banks of the Snail River. The villagers are short and gangly, with thick, red hair, blue-grey eyes and light skin with broad faces, flat noses and narrow eyes. The hunters are horsemen, armed with lances, shields and long daggers. Some horsemen carry staff-slings as well.

Treasure: 380 sp, 880 gp stolen from the coffers of Swiftwater.

Shard, Fighting-Woman Lvl 7: HP 42; AC 3 [16]; Save 8; CL/XP 7/600. Chainmail, shield, lance, long sword. Light skin, black eyes, reddish-blond hair, heavyset and lustful.

1309. In a smoldering clearing you find a dozen charred hovels surrounding what looks like a large, circular barn made of field stone. This was once a dairy, where mechanical milkmaids made delicious cheeses. The dairy was struck by two terrible misfortunes. The first was a fire that roared through the area many years ago. The second was that, unknown to the milkmaids, the cellar where they kept their wheels of sweet cheese harbored brown mold, which, in the presence of heat, spreads rapidly. The mold killed the human owners of the dairy and the milk cows (their forzen corpses remain to this day), but the automatons still go about their business, dragging any mammal they can find into the barn to be milked and freezing them in the process. The milkmaids are bell-shaped, made of bronze and move via wheels in their under-chassis. They have porcelain faces and are painted as though in traditional garb.

Treasure: 600 cp and 500 gp scattered around the hovels and barn.

Milkmaid (10): HD 1+1; AC 4 [15]; Atk 1 weapon (1d8+1); Move 12; Save 17; CL/XP 2/30; Special: Half damage from weapon damage.

1414. An ancient hospice stands in the woods here, surrounded by overgrown medicinal gardens. The hospice looks run down and at first abandoned, but it is inhabited by a small band of monks. The building is constructed atop a grotto containing medicinal springs, the water being bottled and sold as a cure-all (30 gp for a bottle, no medicinal value at all). The hospice was dedicated to Almerla, the goddess of healing. Unfortunately, the hospice and its shrine were dessicrated years ago when the entire population of priests was murdered by a band of assassins. The assassins took over running the place, selling the useless elixirs of spring water and using the fortified abbey as a base of operations for assassinations throughout the Valley of the Hawks. Tarset, Lord Mayor of Swiftwater uses them extensively to maintain his control over the city. The "abbot" is a man called Lachris, and he has under his command a dozen assassins. Almerla's idol still rests in the abandoned chapel. She appears as an inhumanly tall woman with an hour-glass build, unclothed with china-white skin and purple eyes. An alligator curls around the goddess' feet.

Treasure: 3,700 gp and an aventurine worth 9,000 gp. The aventurine is held by the idol of Almerla, and has not been removed for fear of unleashing her fury.

Lachris: HD 6 (30 hp); AC 4 [15]; Atk 1 weapon (1d8 + poison); Move 12; Save 11; CL/XP 7/600; Special: Poisoned weapon,

surprise on 1-3 on 1d6, triple damage on surprise. Chainmail, shield, sword and 2 poisoned daggers. He wears a brass toe ring worth 10 gp.

Assassin: HD 3; AC 6 [13]; Atk 1 weapon (1d8 + poison); Move 12; Save 14; CL/XP 4/120; Special: Poisoned weapon, surprise on 1-3 on 1d6, double damage on surprise.

1418. In a low clearing in the forest, with somewhat swampy ground, there lies a weathered, grey monolith covered in thick vines hung with dazzling, golden grapes. The monolith has sunk into the ground slightly, and now points a bit to the northwest. If the vines are cleared, one will see carvings of dancing satyrs and dryads on the monolith. At the top of each side of the four-sided monolith there is a "green man" carving. If four people touch the faces simulataneously, the ground shudders and a random event occurs.

D6	Event
1-3	People are teleported 1d6+6 hexes away in a random direction (no save).
4-5	The monolith summons 2d6 hostile satyrs.
6	A secret compartment opens, revealing a gilded wreath. When worn on the head, it offers protection from dragons (as a scroll) and causes fey creatures to regard you as a friend.

1522. A fountain of water bubbles from a cliff faced carved in the image of a giant face. The water pools in a depression in the ground. Flesh dipped in the fountain withers into nothingness, but grows back one week later as living (e.g. moveable) ivory.

1602. During the age of the giants, massive creatures called mound monsters came down from the northern tundra, bringing with them frigid winds and turning the prairie into a tundra itself. The mound monsters look something like 50-ft tall stegosaurs with the heads of elephants and long, shovel-like tusks. They have thick, rubbery black skin and spines the color of aged limestone. These mound monsters dug enormous trenches and hollows with their tusks, sifting the soil for their nutrients. The lakes of the northern lake country were mostly formed by these tremendous creatures. Only a few came as far south as the Valley of the Hawks, and were hunted by the ancient giants. When the air turned warmer, most of the mound monsters fled. A few, including one now dwelling in this hex, burrowed into the ground to hibernate until the northern ice spirits again extended their dominion over the Valley of the Hawks. Its existance is marked solely by a tall hill, which the local centaurs believe is a sacred mound. A centaur band led by the venerable Ostan, dwells around the base of the sacred mound and protects it from intruders. It is said that the shrill call of a silver flute will awaken the beast, but the flute in question has been lost for many centuries. The centaurs make wine from wild grapes that acts as a half-powered healing potion but has a chance to cause madness if imbibed too often by non-fey.

Centaurs (12): HD 4; AC 4 [16]; Atk 2 kicks (1d6) and weapon (1d8); Move 18; Save 13; CL/XP 5/240; Special: None.

Ostan: HD 6 (32 hp); AC 4 [16]; Atk 2 kicks (1d6) and weapon (1d8); Move 18; Save 11; CL/XP 7/600; Special: None. Gray hair, brown eyes, big boned and gentle, collects rare coins and knows the vintners art. Hind quarters of a blue roan.

Mound Monster: HD 20 (71 hp); AC 0 [19]; Atk 1 bite (4d6); Move 3; Save 3; CL/XP 30/7600; Special: Brainless, earthquake when it moves, half damage from acid, cold, electricity and fire, swallows foes whole, trample for 4d6 damage).

1608. Here lie the Gardens of Mistress Rho, lovely paths of crushed red stone bordered by tall rushes of brilliantly colored bulbs and tangled trees bearing large, golden pears. Rho is a ghost, a former chatelaine of the ancient city (Hex 1906) who dwelled here in a summer villa. She appears as a beautiful, mature woman with brilliant green eyes, a delicate build and a round face. She is chatty and urbane, but should she permit a young man to kiss her, he will age 1d6 decades in mere seconds. Upon such an occurance, Rho will shriek and she and her lovely gardens will disappear.

1625. An old, run-down abbey of porcelain towers topped by brass cones is nestled beside the river here, amid a veritable garden of rushes, lilies and persimmon trees. The abbey is dedicated to Onorix, the goddess of wealth and governed by Abbot Drute. Drute commands six acolytes and a tribe of 60 lizardmen who fish in the river and protect the abbey in return for silver jewelry (each one wears 10 gp worth of jewelry). The central tower of the abbey is the largest, and houses an imposing idol of Onorix, an athletic looking women with golden hair, beady green eyes (beryls worth 100 gp each), porcelain skin (literally) and a crimson robe covered in interlocking gold circles. The idol carries a brass trumpet which, if blown, summons a minor demon to the abbots service. Drute covets the secrets of the elves and will pay handsomely for information or a prisoner to interogate.

Treasure: Kept in a locked steel chest with a poison needle trap. 1,450 gp and a porcelain urn worth 800 gp containing 7 pounds of cardamon (worth 15 gp per pound).

Drute, Cleric Lvl 9: HP 38; AC 3 [16]; Save 7 (5 vs. paralysis and poison); CL/XP 11/1700; Special: Cast 5th level cleric spells, turn undead. Armor of bronze coins (treat as ring armor +2), shield, mace, holy symbol. Greedy and witty, Drute has blue-grey eyes and black hair. He is fragile-looking, but really quite tough.

Acolyte: HD 1; AC 3 [16]; Atk 1 weapon (1d8); Move 9; Save 17 (15 vs. paralysis and poison); CL/XP 1/15. Special: Turn undead. Chainmail, shield, mace, holy symbol.

1712. A tribe of 200 goblins lives in a dank set of partially flooded catacombs that belonged to a long-gone city of ancient men. The walls of the catacombs are smooth and white and have dozens of secret doors and tunnels and alcoves containing bronze chests containing the ashes and bones of their dead. When opening one of these boxes, there is a 5% chance that it is trapped with poisonous gas (save or 2d6 damage). The water in the catcombs comes from an underground spring, and flows out into the Valley via a tiny cave. The goblins of the catacomb are expert archers. They are brave, but debauched warriors who dwell in extended family units, each led by a swaggering chieftain at odds with his fellows until a fat merchant or pesky adventurers approach the lair.

Treasure: 2,820 sp, 3,070 gp, an amber tortoise worth 200 gp, an olivine worth 800 gp and a large supply of hazelnuts taken from a passing caravan (200 lb, worth 5 sp per pound).

1720. As one enters the craggy uplands through this gorge, they might notice a great deal of rubble strewn about. Sharp eyes will see that the rubble is composed of many hundreds of stone statues. Continuing up the gorge, the ground becomes misty and the footing treacherous until one finally reaches the cave of the resident gorgon.

Gorgon: HD 8 (40 hp); AC 2 [17]; Atk 1 gore (2d6); Move 12; Save 8; CL/XP 10/1400; Special: Breath turns to stone.

1816. A tribe of 22 bugbears live high in these trees in nests of woven sticks. They are led by Kronka, a chief with a harem of 10 females. Kronka is assisted by four sub-chiefs with 4 HD each. The bugbears wield pole arms and javelins and worship a being they call the Warrior Invincible (really an ornate set of Gothic platemail enchanted with a Magic Mouth that utters random invectives they believe are prophecies). The bugbears cultivate a breed of caterpillars that are poisonous to humans but cause them to go into wild hallucinations.

Treasure: 1,120 gp, porcelain candlestick worth 60 gp.

Kronka: HD 5+1 (22 hp); AC 5 [14]; Atk 1 bite (2d4) or weapon (1d8+1); Move 9; Save 14; CL/XP 5/240; Special: Surprise on 1-3 on 1d6.

1906. This windswept hex is home to what the people of the Valley call the "Bones of the Old City". A city of the ancient, golden-skinned men once thrived here, but time and divine vengeance have wiped most of it away, leaving only the steel skeletons of towers and a few cracked domes. The great idol of Kishrdis, the goddess of mining, still stands in the city center, a 50' tall obsidian statue of a short, muscular crone with slitted eyes and lank grey hair. The Old City has two features of interest.

The first, lying on the outskirts of the city, is the College of Tyrie, a fortified monastery of arts and sciences where young men and women are tutored by the clarks of Alcumon, the patron saint of educators and pedagogues. The blessing of Alcumon protects the monastery and holds the unwholesome creatures of the Old City at bay. Her idol depicts a thin woman with a bald head, blue skin and red eyes carrying a large bell on a chain. The College is governed by the Abbess Yourch and employs a dozen priestesses. Yourch is married to the Forgotten One, a bitter deal she made to keep her college in operation. Each fall, she and her priestesses must make a call on the Forgotten One to pay tribute in the form of their brightest young student. These students are experimented on by the Forgotten One, and usually freed to roam the city as mutants (treat as trolls). The monastery treasure is 2,400 cp, 280 gp, a limestone sculpture of a pegasus worth 125 gp and two pieces of rose quartz worth 95 gp each.

Yourch, Cleric Lvl 6: HP 19; AC 9 [10]; Save 10 (8 vs. paralysis and poison); CL/XP 8/800; Special: Cast 4th level cleric spells, turn undead. A fat woman, cautious and considerate, with golden skin and crimson hair.

The other feature of interest is the undercity, a radial network of tunnels and chambers filled with mutated beasts and humans on the outskirts and intelligent giant rats near the center. The rats follow the Forgotten One, a terrible necromancer forced to quit his old castle in Hex 1309 who re-established himself here. His ultimate aim is to rule the Valley of the Hawks eternally as a lich. The Forgotten One's treasure includes 1,800 sp, 3,000 gp, 100 yards of radiant silk worth 10 gp per yard a clutch of eight +1 arrows and large, flawed diamond worth 6,000 gp that he had hoped to use as a phylactery.

Forgotten One, Magic-User Lvl 15: HP 23; AC 9 [10]; Save 5 (3 vs. spells); CL/XP 18/3800; Special: Can cast 7th level magic-user spells. The Forgotten One appears as a pleasant, plump man in simple working togs and wearing bifocals. He carries a silver dagger and a wand of sleep with 10 charges.

1908. In the middle of the prairie, amidst crumbling ruins of an ancient town of stone, is a large pool not unlike an olympic sized pool in form and construction. Bathing in the pool, the pure soul is made more pure – the person's skin will take on a silvery glow for 1 week (per a Light spell) and they will enjoy a +2 bonus to all saving throws. The wicked soul is made more wicked; their skin absorbs light (casting shadowly illumination even in the daytime) and they enjoy a +2 bonus to hit and damage. True neutrals are refreshed, and find themselves thereafter pestered by an invisible cherub and imp on their shoulders who battle noisily (to their target, silently to all others) for their soul until they finally declare for law or chaos.

1918. Kelban is a twisted stone giant shaman who dwells in a large cave complex with three cave bears. Kelban knows a few words of creation and can use them to control the weather and animate stones and trees (treat them as small earth elementals and half-strength treants). Inside his cave he keeps a horde of golden skulls worth 2,000 gp and a copper vat that births 1d4 small oozes each day. He can command the oozes, but they usually wander off after a couple days. At any given time, he has 1d4 random oozes under his command.

Roll	Random Ooze
1	**Black Pudding:** HD 5; AC 6 [13]; Atk 1 attack (2d6); Move 6; Save 12; CL/XP 6/400; Special: Acidic surface, immune to cold, divides when hit with lightning
2	**Gelatinous Cube:** HD 2; AC 8 [11]; Atk 1 attack (1d6); Move 6; Save 13; CL/XP 3/60; Special: Paralysis, immune to lightning and cold
3	**Grey Ooze:** HD 2+2; AC 7 [12]; Atk 1 strike (1d8); Move 1; Save 16; CL/XP 4/120; Special: Acid, immunities
4	**Ochre Jelly:** HD 3; AC 8 [11]; Atk 1 acid-laden strike (2d4); Move 3; Save 14; CL/XP 3/60; Special: Lightning divides creature

Kelban: HD 9+3 (44 hp); AC 0 [19]; Atk 1 club (3d6); Move 6; Save 6; CL/XP 11/1700; Special: Throw boulders for 3d6 damage, animate trees and rocks, control weather.

2019. A lonely mountain here is covered, almost entirely, but bas-relief sculptures of giant faces. Breaking up the scuptures is a tall, abandoned keep beneath an overhang. One can reach the keep by following a treacherous, narrow and often steep trail for the better part of a day. Upon reaching the keep, they will discover no contents other than some over-sized shields and spears and a cluth of fifteen harpies armed with maces.

Harpy: HD 3; AC 7 [12]; Atk 2 talons (1d3) and weapon (1d6); Move 6 (Fly 18); Save 14; CL/XP 4/120; Special: Flies, siren song (charm person).

2022. In the midst of the ruins of a village on a plateau you discover a bleached skeleton wearing green, leather shoes. The shoes, once put on, cannot be removed unless their curse is broken. The shoes force the wearer to make a saving throw or begin dancing a jaunty jig for 1d6 hours, suffering 1d6 lost hit points per hour. At the end of the dance, another save must be made to avoid dancing another 1d6 hours, and so on. The body is surrounded by the shattered remains of musical instruments and wreaths of dried flowers. Feral dogs and cats stalk the empty streets of the village, and a shadowy presence (the shadow of the dead dancer) lurks in a bell tower.

Shadow: HD 3+3 (15 hp); AC 7 [12]; Atk 1 touch (1d4 + Str drain); Move 12; Save 14; CL/XP 4/120; Special: Drains 1 Str with hit, only be harmed by magic weapons.

2121. Buried beneath a mountain with a twisted peak, at the bottom of a deep mine dug by the giants and now devoid of the rare earths for which they delved, lives the gold dragon Iared atop his pile of treasure. Iared ventures from his hiding place once a century to walk (as a man of the ancient race, though dressed not in animal skins but the finery of that bygone civilization) through the terraces and alleys of Swiftwater, enjoying the apple blossom festival and partaking in wild trysts with handsome maidens. At the height of the festival, he appears in the sky in his true form, and seizes said maiden to carry her to his cave as his boon companion for a decade or so until again he feels the siren call of slumber. Before he dozes, he gives his lady fair a large jewel and a silk pennant to proclaim his protection, and sends her back to her people to live out her days as the high priestess of his little shrine, wielding the powers of a 5th level magic-user.

Treasure: 2,270 sp, 3,430 gp, a marble idol of himself worth 1,750, silver medallion worth 90 gp, a collection of 100 peacock feathers, each feather worth 1 gp, and an amethyst worth 7,000 gp.

Iared: HD 12 (96 hp); AC 2 [17]; Atk 2 claws (1d6), bite (3d8); Move 12 (Fly 24); Save 3; CL/XP 15/2900; Special: Fire (cone 90' long, 30' at base) or chlorine breath (50' x 40' x 30'), cast spells as 6th level magic-user.

2206. A wild party of thirty nomads has made camp here in tents of stitched together beetle carapaces. The nomads have golden brown skin, reddish-brown hair that grows thick on their necks, shoulders, arms and back, and purple-blue eyes. They are short and gaunt, and have ugly faces and over-large teeth. The nomads herd giant aphids, milking them for their bitter secretions and fermenting this milk into a chunky beverage that turns them into wild hyenas (treat the nomads as werewolves). The nomads worship Alberni, the diabolical goddess of the moon, who appears as a voluptuous woman with the head of a dog wearing purple armor and carrying a silver disc. A wooden idol of the goddess is carried about by the nomads in a wagon pulled by human slaves. In battle, the wagon's tarp is pulled back to reveal the goddess, sending her followers into a frenzy.

Treasure: 2,500 sp, 900 gp, tiger's eye worth 75 gp.

Nomad: HD 2 + 2; AC 5 [14]; Atk 1 bite (1d6+1); Move 12; Save 13; CL/XP 3/60; Special: Lycanthropy.

2213. The town Swiftwater tumbles down a series of hills to the banks of the river. Swiftwater is the largest settlement in the region, beginning as a trading post of the southmen and grew quickly on the timber trade. The town is constructed on wide terraces that run parallel to the river, each terraced being connected to the others via wide stairs, ramps and pulleys. The citadel occupies a middle position in the town. It is a three-story tower keep constructed of grey stone and flying the arms of the city-state from every parapet. The town is surrounded by a tall wall of grey stone set with many towers and a massive gate flanked by statues of giants carved from green malachite. The town's buildings are mostly constructed of red brick with sloping roofs of beaten copper or slate. The town has no temples and no high priest, but rather a hundred or so competing shrines wherein all the gods of the region are represented by argumentative priests who put on displays of their power and wealth to herd the townsfolk into their shrines to make offerings every time a tragedy occurs. Swiftwater is a bustling center of commerce, its people making a living on the mercenary trade, timber, livestock and the drinking and smoking establishments that line the riverfront.

Swiftwater has three companies of men-at-arms, each of 100 pikemen as its primary defense, along with crossbow-armed town guards and a squadron of 20 chainmail-clad horsemen. The army is under the command of Cunobar, an envoy of the southern city-states.

Swiftwater is governed by Lord Mayor Tarset, a shrewd politician who unwillingly serves his masters in the city-states of the south. Tarset wishes to concentrate his power over the Valley of the Hawks and grow his city on river tolls between the northern lake country and southern coast. With enough wealth and warriors, he can declare himself a palatine noble and rule the Valley of the Hawks as a prince. Tarsets sisters act as his reeves in some of the surrounding villages, and he is advised by Blaith, a scholarly man who served Tarset's father and tutored Tarset as a youth. Swiftwater also boast the services of Thonfur, a dwarven master armorer.

Lord Mayor Tarset, Fighting-Man Lvl 7: HP 39; AC 1 [18]; Save 8. Platemail, shield, long sword +2, silver dagger. Target is a small man with tan skin and auburn hair. He is recently widowed, his wife dying after a brief illness (poison is suspected), **and keeps a fine flock of falcons for hunting.**

Captain Cunobar, Fighting-Man Lvl 6: HP 34; AC 1 [18]; Save 9. Platemail, shield, long sword, dagger. A lean, light-skinned man with mutton chops and a droopy face. Although he appears to be rather thick, his darting blue-grey eyes suggest an active mind. Usually crabby.

Blaith, Sage: HD 1d4 (1 hp). A small, hunched man with pale skin and a round face with a pug nose. His glasses are always drooping and greasy. Innocent and talkative.

Thonfur, Dwarf Armorer: HD 1 (8 hp). Brown skin, short, curly black hair and a beard of black ringlets, steel grey eyes, he is honest and flirtatious.

2216. A tribe of 30 owl-men dwell in the trees here, wielding catch poles and darts. They prey on travelers, selling them to unscrupulous slavers from Swiftwater.

Owl-Men: HD 2; AC 3 [16]; Atk 1 weapon (grapple or 1d6) or 2 talons (1d4); Move 9 (Fly 15); Save 16; CL/XP 3/60; Special: See in all darkness, even magical.

2308. Amidst a field of brown and stunted grass that seems to writhe about independent of the breeze one might (1 in 6 chance) notice the gleam of gunmetal. The dark metal belongs to a crashed ship from beyond the world we know, a ship that brought with it the cursed vampires who now stalk the valley. Several hours of digging reveals a hatch (roll under intelligence to figure out how to open it). The hatch leads into area 1 below.

1 — This long hallway is empty save for several steel doors that resist opening.

2 — On the upper deck, these rooms are either simple cabins or storage closets. Rooms hold a sleeping bubble and weird, greyish mirror. Storage chambers might hold suits of a lightweight silvery material, bulb-shaped helmets of glass or whatever else the Referee deems appropriate. On the lower deck, these chambers contain large weapons that look like cylindrical masses of glass tubes and wires on pedestals. The "cannon" mesh with the wall and while are completely inoperable contain large chunks of crystal worth about 30 gp each. The lower deck is haunted by three wraiths.

Wraith: HD 4 (26, 21, 19 hp); AC 3 [16]; Atk Touch (1d6 + level drain); Move 9; Save 13; CL/XP 6/400; Special: Drain 1 level per hit.

3 — This is the cockpit. It once had a rounded glass canopy, but that has been shattered. The room is now mostly full of soil, though one can make out a circular staircase leading to the lower deck.

4 — This was the engine room. In the center of the room there is something reminiscent of a crystaline accordian in shape that is so bright is dazzles the eyes. A crystaline tube leads from the accordian to the back of the room. If shattered, the "accordian" will release a radiation elemental into the chamber.

Radiation Elemental: HD 8 (31 hp); AC 2 [17]; Atk 1 ray (3d6); Move 30; Save 8; CL/XP 10/1400; Special: Aura of death, only harmed by magical weapons.

2324. Atop a particularly misty, cloudy peak the cloud giant Rhoth has built his fastness, looking down on the surrounding lands as his rightful domain and cursing the petty elves and men for denying him its lordship. Rhoth's household includes his three daughters and a dozen human slaves, as well as a squadron of twenty flying monkeys who serve as his footsoldiers. Rhoth has the look of a great khan in his silks and satins. He has long claws and jutting tusks and eyes

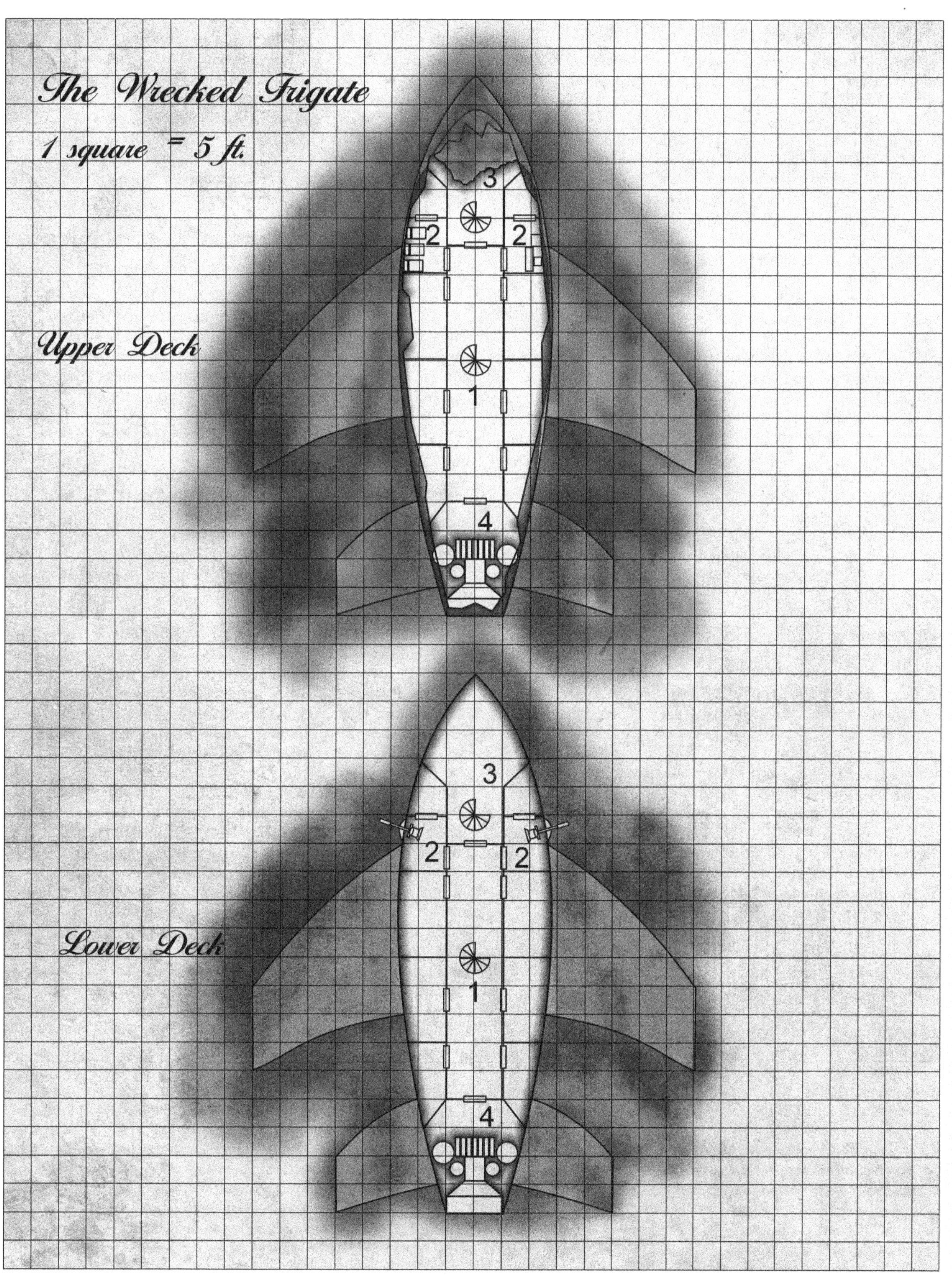
The Wrecked Frigate
1 square = 5 ft.
Upper Deck
3
2
2
1
4
Lower Deck
3
2
2
1
4

as white as ice. Two of Rhoth's daughters, Emryn and Thred, are as cruel and malicious as their father, while the third and youngest daughter, Otmink, is beautiful and kind, and thus despised by her family.

Treasure: 1500 sp, 3000 gp, a garnet worth 450 gp set in a bronze back scratcher (giant-sized) and a serpentine idol worth 95 gp used as a door stop.

Rhoth: HD 12+3 (46 hp); AC 2 [17]; Atk 1 weapon (6d6); Move 15; Save 3; CL/XP 13/2300; Special: Hurl boulders.

Flying Monkey (20): HD 2; AC 5 [14]; Atk Fists (1d6); Move 9 (Fly 12); Save 16; CL/XP 2/30; Special: None.

2421. There are a number of tall, conical spires here topped by large, balancing stones. If the stones are removed, thousands of mechanical locusts will pour from the spires and descend on the Valley of the Hawks, making it a wasteland unless stopped.

2519. The elves of the Winter Court have their stronghold here in a hollow of tangled willows that always seems to be cold and damp. The rotting logs of the hollow support all manner of slime molds and toadstools. Under its glamer, the elf stronghold appears to be a hillock of barren, grey stone. Without illusion, it isn't much better, being a shell keep of large, clumsy grey stones covered in lichens and brown vines. The stronghold is ruled by King Cainn and Queen Wocca and their morbid son Prince Udegion. Twenty pale, gaunt elves live in this place, practicing with their black-feathered arrows and slim swords. Their closeness to the Winter Court has given them the power of wights and a kennel of shadowy hounds to command. The meager grasses around the stronghold are grazed by seven shaggy oxen.

Treasure: 9,660 gp, bag of devouring.

King Cainn: HD 6; AC 5 [14]; Atk 1 sword (1d6 hp + level drain); Move 9; Save 11; CL/XP 8/800; Special: Drains one level, only hit by magic or silver weapons. Wears a brass torque worth 800 gp.

Winter Elf: HD 3; AC 5 [14]; Atk 1 sword (1d6 hp + level drain); Move 9; Save 14; CL/XP 5/240; Special: Drains one level, only hit by magic or silver weapons.

Shadow Hound (10): HD 3+3; AC 7 [12]; Atk Touch (1d4 + Str drain); Move 12; Save 14; CL/XP 4/120; Special: Drains 1 point of Str with hit, only hit by magical weapons.

2704. An old, grey horse wanders this area, grazing on the grasses and accompanied by twenty zombies in leather harnesses and carrying barbed spears. The zombies were under the command of the necromancer Bethnay, whose body is still dragged by the horse after a fall cracked open her skull. The zombies accompany their mute master, waiting for new orders. The remains of Bethnay still hold a treasure map in one boot.

Zombies: HD 2; AC 8 [11]; Atk 1 strike or weapon (1d8); Move 6; Save 16; CL/XP 2/30; Special: Immune to sleep and charm.

2711. The noble paladin Sir Effington maintains a castle in this hex on the edge of the forest. He runs his castle as a hospice and way station for caravans heading to and from Swiftwater, and his soldiers patrol the plains looking for monsters to slay and unfortunates to save. Of course, Effington's men are not as noble as he, and sometimes expect something in return for their services. The castle is constructed of dull, brown stone, which Chauncy has tried to brighten up with multi-colored pennons and shields. Sir Effington's soldiers are heavy footmen who wear chainmail and carry pole arms (glaives). They are mostly impressed peasants and are known for

their love of drink (and Effington runs a dry fief). Sir Effington's elite soldiers are his Paen Company, eight fast riding hussars armed with bolas and hooked swords and riding swift horses. While they are merciful to their defeated foes, they are as strict about discipline as their lord (and he's positively obsessive about it). Effington's fief houses over 300 safe but mildly annoyed peasants who work the nut orchards and keep ponds of scarlet carp. The village is orderly and composed of very clean cottages divided by straight gravel lanes. The village is home to a semi-retired thief named Ambel and has a church overseen by Flisar the Fist. Effington also employs Gwelda of the Golden Eye, a mystic mage skilled in alchemy. Sir Effington is in the process of gathering adventurers for an expedition into the dungeon in 0304.

Treasure: 7,500 gp and a golden holy symbol worth 600 gp hanging in the castle's chapel.

Sir Effington, Fighter Lvl 12: HP 57; AC 1 [18]; Save 4. CL/ XP 12/2000; Platemail, shield, long sword. Fine-boned, very dark skin, silky black hair. Effington is stubborn and obsessive, and stands only 3' 6" tall due to a past encounter with The Forgotten One [Hex 1309]. He has a wyvern mount named Gugeirde that he captured in the far western mountains.

Flisar the Fist, Cleric Lvl 6: HP 24; AC 3 [16]; Save 10 (8 vs. paralysis and poison); CL/XP 8/800; Special: Can cast 4th level spells, turn undead. Wears chainmail under his white robes, carries a shield with a red cross and a rusty mace. Flisar has chocolate skin, a heart-shaped face, long, gray hair and amber eyes. He is aggressive and out-going, and known for his mean right hook. He worships Murchuter, the god of truth, who appears as a man with black skin and golden, almond-shaped eyes.

Gwelda of the Golden Eye, Magic-User Lvl 4: HP 8; AC 9 [10]; Save 12 (10 vs. spells); CL/XP 5/240; Special: Can cast 2nd level spells. Passive and charming, she records her spells on pottery. Has shoulder-length, wavy blond hair, a plain face with many laugh lines and a sparkling voice. Gwelda loves children and pines away for Sir Effington, who seems oblivious to her dreams of holy matrimony. Gwelda is a skilled alchemist.

Ambel the Thief, Fighter Lvl 4: HP 14; AC 5 [14] in armor; Save 11; CL/XP 4/120. Ring mail and shield, throwing axe and short sword. Ambel has dark brown skin, hazel eyes and a wiry build. He is a bit of a tavern philosopher, and newly married to an olive-skinned woman named Valda. Valda is not great beauty, but she owns a nice cottage and a pond full of fat carp.

2717. This hex holds the remnants of a natural earth bridge that once spanned the river. What remains appear to be popular with the giant hawks of the region, for the congregate here night and day and do their best to dissuade visitors. On the bottom of the river, directly beneath the center of the now long-gone span, is a globe of chalcedony that empowers its possessor to control the giant hawks as a wicked cleric controls the undead.

2806. This large village of northman spear fishers is ruled by a coterie of vampires under the command of the countess Jordelia and her brood. Jordelia has resided in the village since she and her people first came to the Valley of the Hawks, and after centuries has left her mark upon the place. Once a simple village of wattle & daub huts, it is not composed entirely of stone pavilions that block the sun. Set upon a steep hill, the village proceeds in terraced steps, seemingly being dozens of little buildings stacked upon one another in an untidy pile. The people tolerate the vampires, for what else is there to do; they mostly leave them to their own devices, feeding on people in turns and taking care not to spread their malady. In return, they protect the village. The village milita consists of 10 vampires and perhaps 20 giant bats, as well as three undead ogres encased on plate armor and wielding great mauls. The human spokesman is called Brences, a merchant with bright, amber eyes and a ready wit. The vampires in Hex 2407 were exiled from here after a power struggle.

Treasure: 12,800 gp, sapphire worth 3,200 gp, sunstone worth 1,550 gp hidden in the home of Brences under a loose floor tile.

Jordelia: HD 9; AC 2 [17]; Atk 1 bite (1d10 + level drain); Move 12 (Fly 18); Save 6; CL/XP 12/2000; Special: See monster description. Fair skin, grey eyes, long, auburn hair in ringlets.

Vampires: HD 7; AC 2 [17]; Atk 1 bite (1d10 + level drain); Move 12 (Fly 18); Save 9; CL/XP 10/1400; Special: See monster description. Pallid complexion, silver hair, pink eyes.

Giant Bats: HD 4; AC 7 [12]; Atk 1 bite (1d10); Move 4 (Fly 18); Save 13; CL/XP 5/240; Special: 10% chance of disease.

2822. Out of the dense canopy of oak rises a blood red obelisk. At the foot of the obelisk there is a simple hut of wattle & daub with a silvery roof of birch bark. In the hut dwells the fair Omissa, gambler, swordswoman and ne'er-do-well, and exemplar of Chaos who has taken to the life of a hermit and sometime proselytizer. The hut is a simple affair, containing a down mattress covered in black vevlet and surrounded by silk curtains of mauve and grey and a chest of mahogany bound in bronze and locked and trapped with an excretion of chaos that, should it prick one's finger, will polymorph the would-be thief into a random animal of small size and questionable utility. Inside the chest Omissa keeps a map purporting to show the Seven Seals of Alkmene and describing how they must be attuned to permit the entrance of Things Undreamed into the world. Omissa is usually to be found outside her hut, playing with a deck of cards or oiling her singing sword. She happily takes up games of chance and half-heartedly picks apart the Lawful beliefs of others, though she shows no particular hostility toward worshippers of Law.

Treasure: Map of the Seven Seals, 2,200 cp, 740 sp, 440 gp, a bronze aquamanile worth 300 gp.

Omissa, Fighting-Woman Lvl 8: HP 44; AC 1 [18]; Save 7; CL/ XP 8/800. Platemail, longsword +1/+3 vs. elementals, shield emblazoned with a scowling medusa. Has golden-brown skin, lean and muscular with lightning blue eyes and short, curly hair of silver.

2911. Almost without the adventurers being aware of it, the wooded landscape changes toward the center of this hex. Where once there was a floor of fern and moss, now there is ancient grey pavement stamped with the image of a double-headed unicorn. Where once great elms scraped at the sky, there are now grey pillars, heaps of stacked cylinders looming precariously over the grey tiles. Atop the pillars are grotesques in grey, eyes lifted toward the heavens. In the center of this "petrified" forest there is a deep pool of black water that seems to heave and sigh as folk come near it. When light strikes this pool from the Moon, it becomes phosphorescent white and one can glimpse nymphs draped in garlands of pink blossoms beckoning the visitor to enter. Those who do find themselves in the tangled fungal forests of the Moon, and find their hosts not at all what they appeared to be. Of course, to get close to the pool, one must first deal with the aforementioned grotesque gargoyles.

Gargoyles (20): HD 4; AC 5 [14]; Atk 2 claws (1d3), bite (1d4), horn (1d6); Move 9 (Fly 15); Save 13; CL/XP 6/400; Special: Fly.

2914. The plains here are roamed by dozens of giant beetles (1-2 on 1d6 chance of encounters with 1d6 giant beetles), and are thus also studded with massive balls of animal dung holding their incubating eggs.

3018. A small village of coarse, loutish peasants lives here in brick longhouses surrounded by an earthen rampart with moat and three brick towers set into the rampart. The peasants are of northern stock, with reddish-brown hair. Unlike their kinsmen, they dress in woollen hoses and shapeless tunics. The peasants once mined the surrounding area for corundums, but now herd sheep and giant tortoises and grow fields of amaranth. The village is defended by 10 men-at-arms wearing ring armor and carrying tortoise-shell shields and wicked looking clubs. The village is laxly governed by Magillee, an ex-river pirate who, with his aforementioned thugs, decided to settle in the village when he grew tired of his life of piracy. Magillee is married to a local beauty who lords it over her kinsmen bedecked in strings of pearls and silver (worth 100 gp). The couple have several ill-mannered children.

Magillee, Fighting-Man Lvl 6: HP 48; AC 5 [14]; Save 9; CL/XP 6/400. Ring mail, shield, long sword and throwing axe. Magillee is brash and loyal to a fault. He has tawny skin, steel grey eyes and long, brown hair. Tall and thin, his face has become sallow and drawn from smoking black lotus in a long, clay pipe.

3121. A giant boar the locals have named Father Lobald, has wandered these woods for many years, resisting all attempts by the elven hunters to kill it. Any person who can claim the head as a trophy will have their charisma adjusted by +4 (to a max of 18) in this region for the purposes of attracting henchmen and hirelings.

Father Lobald: HD 6+6 (54 hp); AC 5 [14]; Atk 1 gore (4d6); Move 18; Save 11; CL/XP 4/120; Special: Continue attacks 4 rounds after death.

3210. Hidden by tall, overarching trees there is a tower of translucent crystal that is home to Djak, a dwarf lord who is marshalling an army that he believes will conquer the entire Valley of Hawks and make him a king. The tower is 30-ft wide and 50-ft tall and was constructed by some unknown wizard as a greenhouse. It still contains terraces of exotic plants and the grounds are covered with living topiaries that willingly serve Djak so long as he keeps the lawn weeded and gives them some mulch now again. Djak commands 40 dwarf warriors known for their heroism and their deadly use of heavy flails. His also has 10 elite warriors who wear long, sable coats and wield iron staves. These men, the Sable Company by name, really consider themselves attached to the stronghold, not Djak.

Djak's army is gathered from throughout the Valley of the Hawks and beyond, and now numbers nearly 400 soldiers. Their camp surrounds the stronghold and their presence is irritating the local elves and fey. Assisting Djak in his plans of conquest are Sicio the Sardonic, a priest of chaos, and Meron the Fat, a magician of ill-repute in the region.

Treasure: 34,000 sp (to pay the troops), 1,620 gp.

Djak, Dwarf Lvl 9: HP 56; AC 1 [18]; Save 6; CL/XP 9/1100. Wears platemail and carries shield and heavy flail and has a potion of animal control. Djak is a porcine, moody dwarf with brown hair, amber eyes and chocolate brown skin. He is brash and irritable.

Sicio the Sardonic, Cleric Lvl 6: HP 24; AC 6 [13]; Move 12; Save 10 (8 vs. paralysis and poison); CL/XP 8/800; Special: Can cast 4th level spells and command undead. Sicio is selfish and soft-spoken with short, grey hair, green eyes and black skin. Carries a buckler and mace. He is big-boned with a round, cheerful face. His body is covered in mystic symbols that protect him as well as leather armor. Sicio worships Zimpaxa, a minor chaos-deity that appears as a voluptuous crone with tentacles in place of her hair and prismatic eyes. Zimpaxa's skin is a tableau of constantly changing images like multi-colored tattooes.

Meron the Fat, Magic-User Lvl 4: HP 8; AC 9 [10]; Save 12 (10 vs. spells); CL/XP 5/240; Special: Can cast 2nd level spells.

Meron is grossly obese and has light skin, a small-featured, delicate face, long, light brown hair and grey-green eyes. He is aggressive and grumpy and a former apprentice of the Forgotten One.

3318. An old temple of the snake people rests in this hex, obscured by bulging, tangled black oaks and clinging vines covered with delicate white blossoms that smell of death. The temple is constructed of serpentine that gives off a ghostly glow in the dead of night. The upper temple is an oddly shaped building about 50 feet long and 40 feet wide with no discernable entrance. A secret door obscured by vines and activated by pressing a stone set above the door leads into area 1. All surfaces inside the temple are composed of slate-grey stone with serpentine highlights.

1 — The walls of this chamber are decorated with runes of chaos proclaiming the grandeur of the snake people and their gods, and warning against plundering the confines of the temple. Terracotta bowls in the room hold 600 sp and 200 gp.

2 — One step in the stairs leading into this room is a trigger, releasing heavy stones on the heads of intruders. A saving throw must be passed to avoid 2d6 points of damage. The walls of the room are covered in wavy bas-relief sculpture that is hard on the eyes and gives one a queasy feeling. A bronze sarcophagus in the center of the room is not trapped, and holds a bronze ring that, if pulled, opens the secret door.

3 — A weird contraption of conical tubes and spheres in the center of this room is capable of turning bits of flesh or blood into gangs of 1d12 reptilian homunculi. The homunculi attack anyone in the room, attempting to feed their bodies into the contraption to make more of their kind. A discarded backpack in one corner holds 800 sp.

Homunculus: HD 2; AC 6 [13]; Atk 1 bite (1d3 + sleep); Move 6 (Fly 20); Save 16; CL/XP 3/60; Special: Bite causes sleep.

4 — A massive cobra with alabaster scales, easily 30 feet long with a body 4-ft in diameter, is curled up in this room asleep. Approximately 10,000 silver pieces are scattered about. The serpent has a taste for wine.

Alabaster Cobra: HD 14; AC 3 [16]; Atk 1 bite (2d6 + poison); Move 9; Save 3; CL/XP 15/2900; Special: Poison requires a save to avoid a lingering death.

5 — This long chamber has a long, serpentine altar in its center, stained by centuries of blood-letting. A small band of troglodyte priests have persisted in this temple for centuries, living on the waters of the fountain in area 8. A secret cache in the altar holds pentagonal key that, inserted in a hole in the wall of the alcove to the east, opens the secret door. The troglodytes wear ritual arm bands of electrum worth a total of 70 gp. If the troglodytes notice the adventurers tangling with the alabaster serpent, they will attempt to blend into the serpentine walls and attack any living intruders with surprise.

Troglodytes (5): HD 2 (11, 10, 10, 10, 8 hp); AC 4 [15]; Atk 2 claws (1d3), bite (1d4+1) or weapon (1d8); Move 12; Save 16; CL/XP 3/60; Special: Stench, chameleon skin.

6 — Twenty troglodyte warriors live in this dank, mildewed auditorium. They will respond to noises in area 5 or 8. Three of the troglodytes are armed with staffs topped by copper balls that generate 2d6 points of electricity damage and force victims to pass a saving throw or be stunned for 1d4 rounds.

Troglodytes (20): HD 2 (8 hp each); AC 4 [15]; Atk 2 claws (1d3), bite (1d4+1) or weapon (1d8); Move 12; Save 16; CL/XP 3/60; Special: Stench, chameleon skin.

7 — This inner sanctum holds a large, serpentine idol of a goddess with the head and torso of a medusa, six long arms and the lower body of a coiled serpent. Each hand grasps a gold sphere worth 25 gp. Set into the ceiling are six trap doors holding mummified snake men. Any attempt to molest the idol will cause the trapdoors to open and release the mummies, possibly on top of an adventurer (1 in 20 chance for each adventurer in the room).

Mummies (6): HD 6+4 (30 hp each); AC 3 [16]; Atk 1 fist (1d12); Move 6; Save 11; CL/XP 7/600; Special: Rot, hit only by magic weapons.

8 — This room contains a bubbling fountain of sulphurous, yellow liquid. Drinking the liquid allows a creature to live for one year without the need for food or water, and without aging, if a saving throw is passed. Otherwise, the imbiber loses 2d6 points of damage and become nauseous for 1 turn.

9 — This large room is a weird sort of "decompression chamber". The snake men who once lived in the region were visitors from another world, a blasted world of fire and brimstone and poisonous air. By spending a week in this room, they could acclimate themselves to the climate and survive for several weeks here before having to return to their own world. The room contains stone couches and shelves filled with leathery scrolls branded with chaotic runes (reading material), as well as a game that looks similar to chess. Once the secret door is closed, the room seals and proves almost impossible to exit. Slowly, day by day, the air in the room becomes more and more poisonous. A creature that manages to make a saving throw each day does not succumb to the poison, and in fact can survive in the sulphurous air for several weeks. Those who fail two rolls succumb to the poison and die. At the end of one week, the chamber shifts all inside it to the alien world of the snake men.

3411. A den of twelve giant beavers has dammed the river here, blocking the movement of river boats and flooding the area a bit. Folk trying to portage around the dam are being shaken down by the intelligent creatures for tolls. So far, they have amassed 4,590 sp, 200 gp and 11 barrels of wine (30 gallons in each, weigh 250 lb, worth 9 gp each.

Giant Beaver: HD 4+1; AC 7 [12]; Atk 2 claws (1d3), 1 bite (1d6); Move 9; Save 13; CL/XP 4/120; Special: Hug.

3422. An old raft is floating down the river, carrying two brain-eating zombies, one a gray-skinned man with several bites out of his torso, and the other a teenaged boy lacking most of his skin. The two are mindlessly heading down the river. The zombies have no treasure other than an old haversack containing a few coppers and a corncob pipe.

Zombies: HD 2 (9, 6 hp); AC 8 [11]; Atk 1 strike (1d8); Move 6; Save 16; CL/XP 2/30; Special: Immune to sleep and charm.

3605. A small village of ancient men in his hex is plagued by pixies. The woodsmen live in leather tents surrounded by a thicket. They are tall and thin, with golden skin, reddish-brown hair and long noses. The men are bison riders, capable of communicating with and controlling not only their bisons but all mammals (per charm monster and speak with animals). They wield throwing clubs called knobkerries and long, serrated daggers and wear leather armor. The bison riders, there are 25 warriors in the band, are commanded by a barbaric woman called Elobara, a changeling elf. The villagers enjoy the labors of Tyffred, an ebony skinned armorer who crafts their armor and weapons.

Elobara, Elf Lvl 8: HD 8d6+16 or 8d6-8 (47 or 25 hp); AC 7 [12] or 9 [10]; Save 7/8; CL/XP 8/800; Special: As magic-user, can cast 4th level spells, darkvision to 60-ft, 4 in 6 chance to find secret doors, immune to charm person and sleep. Lanky woman

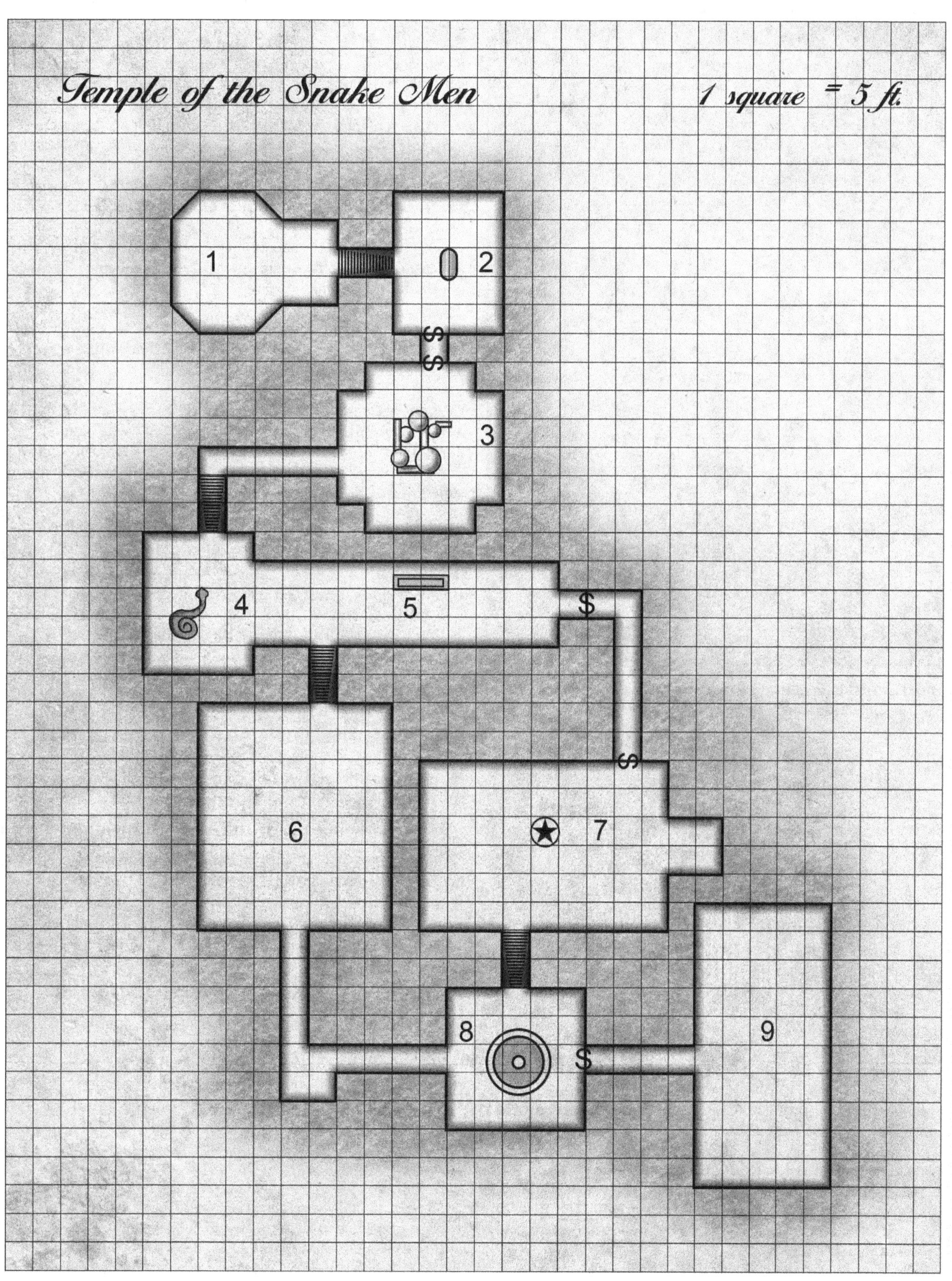

Temple of the Snake Men
1 square = 5 ft.
1
2
3
4
5
6
7
8
9

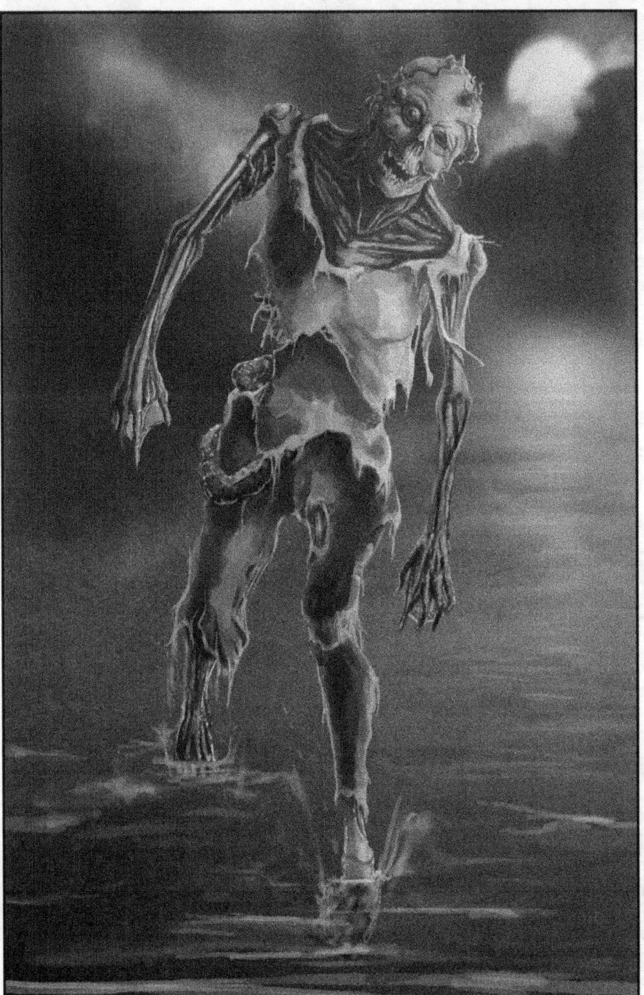

with tawny skin and a wild face, curly red hair and green eyes. She is foul tempered and vulgar.

3708. This large village of southmen is set a couple miles away from the river, and connected to it via a gravel-filled gully that only rarely floods. The village is surrounded by an earthen rampart and dry moat, and consists of several dozen houses of dried, mud brick. The villagers are quarrymen, quarrying a large deposit of granite and a smaller limestone deposit and shipping the blocks down the river. The miners are lanky and quarrelsome, with pale skin and reddish hair and bluish eyes. They wear short capes, wide-brimmed hats and loose trousers in shades of red and orange. Reeve Finla maintains order with 60 ruthless men-at-arms armed with dirks and daggers and renowned for their wanton cruelty. Cabridan, a minor sage, well versed in minerology and the epic poetry of the ancient men, works as Finla's clark. The village boasts a large tavern known for its ginger beer, sweet yeast bread and generous servings of roasted cane rat and horseradish.

Finla, Reeve: HD 4 (7 hp); AC 3 [16]; Atk 1 weapon (1d8); Move 9; Save 13; CL/XP 4/120. A black haired, blue-eyed woman, muscular with a broad, handsome face. Charming and argumentative, she is a fine dancer.

Cabridan, Sage: HD 1d4 (2 hp); AC 9 [10]. A plump, light-skinned man with short, curly brown hair. He is serious about magic and poetry, but has no talent at either endeavor. He is married to Bennorye, a kindly, saintly woman, and has one son, Orance, by her.

3712. Sir Eolan, a hoary old crusader, constructed a tower keep at the bend of the river fifty years ago, and still maintains the peace in the area. He is a kindly old man, but his dedication to honesty sometimes makes him seem rude. Many years ago he lost his lady-love Jordelia to the depredations of vampires, and she now rules over the village in Hex 2806. For decades he has avoided dealing with the vampires, and regrets it mightily.

Eolan's keep is constructed of granite, overlooking the Great River. The hills surrounding the keep have many small platinum deposits, and the hafling miners who live under Eolan's banner work the mines and grow crops within sight of the keep. A sturdy old granite landing allows river boats to dock at the keep. Eolan's forty soldiers are canny halfling woodsmen armed with falchions and slings. Led by strict, black robed warrior-priests, the halflings are quite formidable. Besides the halflings, Eolan commands a corps of eight elite fighting-men armed with halberds and wearing platemail.

Treasure: 640 sp, 1,190 gp, silver belt worth 10 gp – a keepsake of the fair Jordelia.

Halfling Woodsman: HD 1d6; AC 7 [12]; Atk 1 weapon (1d6); Move 6; Save 18; CL/XP B/10; Special: +1 to hit with sling, surprise on 1-3 on 1d6.

Eolan, Fighting-Man Lvl 10: HP 42; AC 1 [18]; Save 5; CL/XP 10/1400. Platemail, shield, long sword, dagger. Eolan is a northman with hazel eyes and a heavy build. Despite his holy manners, he has an obsession with gambling, and reacts with spite towards those who best him.

Dhaida, Cleric Lvl 4: HP 16; AC 1 [18]; Save 12 (10 vs. paralysis and poison); CL/XP 5/240; Special: Can cast 2nd level spells, turn undead. Platemail, shield, mace, holy symbol. Dhaida is rotund, with a craggy face and gray-green eyes. She is ill-tempered and difficult to work with, but does a fine job as Eolan's captain of the guard. Dhaida worships Valina, the goddess of wildlife, who appears as a tall maiden with pine-green hair and china-white skin in a gray tunic carrying a bronze bell.

Wigibet, Magic-User Lvl 3: HP 6; AC 9 [10]; Save 13 (11 vs. spells); CL/XP 4/120; Special: Can cast 2nd level spells. Slender, tawny-skinned woman, with a bland face and blue eyes. Wigibet is irresponsible and bossy. Wears rust-colored robes and carries a slate and chalk.

3723. A large village of northman cattle herders as sprung up in his hex around a series of ancient, geometric fountains. The fountains were constructed in a large, paved square of speckled blue stone, and apparently served as the center piece of a lost settlement. The new villagers have constructed timber longhouses and a wooden palisade, letting their cattle graze on the prairie with only a few horsemen to protect them. The palisade is large enough to house their 200 head of cattle if danger threatens.

The villagers are a deceitful lot, scheming and untrustworthy. They maintain a militia of 50 pikemen, all clever but cruel warriors, and have been successful in resisting the dominations of the southmen, partly thanks to the magic of the fountains (see below). The village is ruled by Theki, the Iron Baron and enjoys the services of an alchemist named Ealsa, who came to the village to study the fountains. The captain of the pikemen is named Ressenald.

The fountains are three in number and carved from colored stone. Each fountain imbues an imbiber with magical abilities that last for one day. Imbibing from a fountain again before one month has passed is poisonous (save or die instantly). The first fountain is triangular in shape, carved from lapis lazuli and decorated with triangles. The second is square in shape, carved from green malachite and decorated with squares. The final fountain in pentagonal in shape, carved from purple porphyry and decorated with pentagons. The effects of each fountain is random:

Roll	Triangle (D4)	Square (D6)	Pentagon (D12)
1	Cannot touch (or be touched) by metal; it passes through body with no effect	Age 10 years (permanent)	Blindness
2	Can fire death ray once per hour	Cause serious wounds by touch (once per hour)	Prime attribute improves by 1
3	Magic resistance 50%	Giant strength	ESP
4	Polymorphed into random monster of same HD	Cast lightning bolt 1/hour	Invisibility
5	—	Only harmed by silver or magic weapons	Immune to fear
6	—	Lose 1d6 points of Strength (permanent)	Detect invisibility
7	—	—	Immune to disease
8	—	—	Immune to magic missiles
9	—	—	Immune to poison
10	—	—	Bless effect (as spell)
11	—	—	AC improves by 2 points
12	—	—	Gender changes

Theki: HD 3 (11 hp); AC 1 [18]; Atk 1 sword (1d8); Move 12 (unarmored); Save 14; CL/XP 3/60; Special: None. Platemail, shield, curved long sword, dagger. Has a fencer's physique, sharp-featured face, secretive and moody.

Ealsa, Magic-User Lvl 1: HP 2; AC 9 [10]; Save 15 (13 vs. spells); CL/XP 2/30; Special: Can cast 1st level spells, has 1d3 random potions for sale, 500 gp each. Acid-stained robes of maroon, pack of herb and reagents, silver dagger. Romantic and willful, mocha skin, black hair and brown eyes, with a sharp-featured face. She has a young son named Garls.

Ressenald: HD 5 (25 hp); AC 1 [18]; Atk 1 weapon (1d8+1); Move 12 (unarmored); Save 12; CL/XP 5/240; Special: Troops are +1 to save vs. fear. Platemail, pike, long sword, dagger. Irresponsible and assertive, he is a man of the old race with golden skin, black eyes and flaming red hair. He is married to a local woman and has several children.

3802. A fortified waystation used by caravaneers has recently been taken by a tribe of ten sabre-toothed ogres with dull, blackish green skin. Those humans they left alive have been turned into chained

serving people for the chieftain, Zargus and his bride, the mysterious White Woman, who controls his moods with her soothing stories and silver flute. The ogres are lotus-eaters, and often in a stupor, but the din of battle awakens a terrible fury in them (e.g. surprised on a roll of 1-4 on 1d6, but thereafter they fight at +2 to hit and damage). The waystation consists of a low, shell keep (like a stone donut) with a tunnel entrance guarded by murder holes and an iron portcullis, and a large central courtyard sporting a well and scarlet tarps providing shade. The waystation has a good collection of supplies (iron rations, rope, etc) that have been left untouched by the ogres. The waystations shrine to Xevus, the god of light and patron of travelers, has been desecrated and turned into a meat locker, currently holding the dismembered bodies of fifteen humans. Xevus' idol shows a tall, blue skinned man with four arms and the feathered wings of a hawk. His head is covered in hawk feathers and he carries a stiletto in each hand. An ancient priest of Xevus was interred under the floor, and the desecration of the shrine has raised his ire; when he finally rises from his grave, a terrible vengeance will surely be wrought on all within reach.

Treasure: 500 cp, 2,700 gp, terracotta chalice worth 85 gp, brass choker worth 2 gp.

Ogres: HD 4+1; AC 5 [14]; Atk 1 axe (1d10+1) or bite (1d6); Move 9; Save 13; CL/XP 4/120; Special: None.

Zargus: HD 6+1; AC 3 [16]; Atk 1 axe (1d12+1) or bite (1d6+1); Move 9; Save 11; CL/XP 6/400; Special: None.

White Woman: HD 3 (14 hp); AC 9 [10]; Atk 1 silver dagger (1d4); Move 12; Save 14; CL/XP 4/120; Special: Can cast magic-user and anti-cleric spells of 3rd level and lower, one per round. The White Woman looks as though she is formed entirely of ivory, including her eyes, teeth and mouth, with the exception of her platinum blond hair.

3910. A village of dour yeomen is nestled in a wooded valley here, protected by a thicket of iron-hard brambles and a dry moat studded with wooden spikes. The villagers have skin as black as night, pale blond hair and almond-shaped eyes of green. They wear the costume typical of the northmen, but more exagerated with flared sleeves and colored in bright reds and purples. The village consists of a few dozen timber longhouses built along the remnants of an ancient road paved in pale, yellow stones. Two large, granite cisterns provide water for the villagers, with their crops of cucumbers, hot peppers and soy relying on rainfall. The villagers are unfriendly and seem nervous, and indeed have good reason to be an in ill temper, as their peace has been disrupted by the arrival of the vampire count Kardofo, the loser in a recent power struggle with his countess, Jordelia [Hex 2806]. Kardofo has taken residence in the root cellar behind the home of the village mayor, Tamosirus (4 hp), and has already turned the mayor's wife, Haimonna, into his willing bride. Ten other villagers have been turned, and now patrol the village at night wielding long, bronze daggers and enforcing their master's new order. Tamosirus and the other peasants fear to move against them, and will do their best to discourage visitors from hanging about. About a mile south of the village there lives an old wise woman, a hermit named Dotty skilled with herb and tincture. Dotty lives with her "imaginary friend" Rex, an invisible stalker bound to her not by spell but by a rare act of kindness. The vampires fear Rex and have left Dotty alone. Dotty is aware of their presence in the neighborhood, and is working feverishly to concoct a plan to remove them.

Treasure: 3500 sp, 190 gp, a wooden flask of red dragon blood, flask worth 55 gp, blood worth 1,000 gp.

Kardofo: HD 8 (30 hp); AC 2 [17]; Atk 1 bite (1d10 + level drain); Move 12 (Fly 18); Save 8; CL/XP 10/1400; Special: See monster description.

Haimonna: HD 7 (28 hp); AC 2 [17]; Atk 1 bite (1d10 + level drain); Move 12 (Fly 18); Save 9; CL/XP 9/1100; Special: See monster description.

Vampire Thugs: HD 7; AC 2 [17]; Atk 1 bite (1d10 + level drain); Move 12 (Fly 18); Save 9; CL/XP 9/1100; Special: See monster description.

Dotty, Magic-User Lvl 5: HP 9; AC 9 [10]; Save 10; CL/XP 6/400; Special: Can cast 3rd level spells. Dusky skin, with black hair tied in pink ribbons and deep, brown eyes. Willowy of build and pot-bellied, she has a round, cheerful face. Dresses in a tattered, patchwork house coat with many pockets.

Rex: HD 8 (54 hp); AC 3 [16]; Atk 1 bite (4d4); Move 12; Save 8; CL/XP 9/1100; Special: Invisible, flies.

New Monsters

Automaton

Automata are the creations of the ancient elves; they were used as labor and as soldiers. Automata are intelligent creatures, but they are not truly alive; that is to say, they are not subject to poison or energy drain and do not need to eat, breath or sleep. The secret of creating automata is long lost. Those that survive into the modern day are quite ancient. Automata are so strong they deal +1 damage with each hit. Each automaton was created by hand; the ancient elves didn't use assembly lines. Thus, each automaton is a unique creation and they can take a multitude of forms. Though automata are physically genderless, they may have personalities that are either masculine or feminine.

Automaton: HD 1+1; AC 4 [15]; Atk 1 weapon (1d8+1); Move 12; Save 17; CL/XP 2/30; Special: Ignore critical hits 25% of the time.

Elemental - Radiation

The radiation elementals are usually to be found flitting about stars, though they sometimes congregate on the planes of fire or earth to harass the locals. They appear as shimmering clouds of motes. Radiation elementals emit an aura of withering death (saving throw or suffer 1d6 points of burn damage and 1 point of constitution damage) and can direct searing rays that inflict 3d6 points of damage.

Radiation Elemental: HD 8; AC 2 [17]; Atk 1 ray (3d6); Move 30; Save 8; CL/XP 10/1400; Special: Aura of death, only harmed by magical weapons.

Kill-Bunny

Kill-bunnies dwell in pastoral settings in large burrow complexes. They resemble 3-ft tall, bipedal rabbits with a murderous gleam in their eyes. Kill-bunnies wear whatever pieces of armor they have taken from victims, usually amounting to ring mail. About 30% carry wooden shields. Kill-bunnies wield short swords, spears and throwing axes in combat. A kill-bunny's lightning reflexes give it a 1 point bonus to AC and saving throws and allows it to make two attacks per round. Whenever a kill-bunny inflicts maximum damage from an attack, it fights for the rest of the combat with a +1 bonus to hit and damage.

Kill-bunny warrens are ruled by 3 HD chieftains. Chieftains keep harems of females who are skilled as thieves and capable of fascinating creatures with their dances. Some warrens include a shaman of "The Beast", the savage deity of the kill-bunnies. The Beast is a deity of wanton slaughter, celebrated with blood sacrifice and quaint folk dances.

Kill-Bunny: HD 1; AC 5 [14]; Atk 1 bite (1d3) or 1 weapon (1d6); Move 15; Save 17; CL/XP 2/30; Special: Lightning reflexes, murderous rage.

Hex Crawl Chronicles: Valley of the Hawks is written under version 1.0a of the Open Game License. As of yet, none of the material first appearing in **Hex Crawl Chronicles: Valley of the Hawks** is considered Open Game Content.

www.ingramcontent.com/pod-product-compliance
Lightning Source LLC
Chambersburg PA
CBHW081329090726

47907CB00010B/2429